She ached with a need for fulfillment

"Has any other man ever made you feel like this?" Slade demanded huskily, lifting his head and studying the pleasure obvious on Chelsea's face. "Has he?" he repeated forcefully, anger mingling with passion.

With a jolt Chelsea felt herself come back to earth. She shivered, sickened by both her own behavior and Slade's egotistical desire to arouse within her something she had felt for no one else.

She forced herself to go limp in his arms, noting with satisfaction the darkening in Slade's eyes as he felt her reaction. At least he had not realized that she loved him, Chelsea thought in relief.

"What's wrong?" she goaded. "Are you wondering how you compare? Would you like a rating on a scale of one to ten?"

PENNY JORDAN
is also the author of these

Harlequin Presents

Many of these books are available at your local bookseller.

For a free catalog listing all titles currently available,
send your name and address to:

HARLEQUIN READER SERVICE
1440 South Priest Drive, Tempe, AZ 85281
Canadian address: Stratford, Ontario N5A 6W2

PENNY JORDAN

JORDAN

rescue operation

Harlequin Books

TORONTO • NEW YORK • LOS ANGELES • LONDON
AMSTERDAM • PARIS • SYDNEY • HAMBURG
STOCKHOLM • ATHENS • TOKYO • MILAN

Harlequin Presents first edition June 1983
ISBN 0-373-10602-5

Original hardcover edition published in 1983
by Mills & Boon Limited

CHAPTER ONE

CHELSEA frowned thoughtfully as she parked her small car carefully behind her sister's BMW. Ann had sounded worried and anxious on the telephone, unusually so, and she sighed a little as she slid long slender legs out of her car. Parenthood brought many perils, if Ann was to be believed, but none more burdensome than those engendered by a seventeen-year-old daughter.

As she had expected she found her sister in her large modern kitchen busily engaged in mixing fruit in a huge bowl.

'Cake for tomorrow,' Ann told her, reaching out automatically to slap away her hand as Chelsea filched a small amount of the raw mixture. 'You're as bad as Kirsty,' she complained, tempering the criticism with a warm kiss on her sister's cheek, as she added, 'Thanks for coming. Did I drag you away from anything important?'

'Only a sixteenth-century chair cover,' Chelsea replied humorously, referring to her work as a restorer of mediaeval embroidery. 'And speaking of Kirsty, what's the problem this time? Not threatening to run off with her favourite pop singer again, is she?'

Ann Stannard shot her sister an exasperated glance. With the fourteen years' difference in their age, Ann sometimes felt more like Chelsea's mother than her sister. Their parents had died

5

when Ann was just twenty-two and on the brink of marriage to Ralph Stannard, and for all her teasing of her sister, Chelsea never forgot Ralph's generosity in giving his orphaned sister-in-law a home. It couldn't have been easy, she recognised from the vantage viewpoint of twenty-six, for the newly married pair to make a precocious and inquisitive teenager welcome.

Kirsty was the Stannards' only child, a spirited and attractive teenager, currently still at school, but as Chelsea well knew, rebelliously determined to leave just as soon as she possibly could.

'She's not still got this bee in her bonnet about becoming an actress, has she?' Chelsea queried.

'I wish that was all we had to contend with. I'm afraid it's far more serious than that. We're both at our wits' end, Chelsea. You're our last hope. You've always been so close to her. Ralph and I were hoping you could make her see sense . . .'

'About what?'

'About Slade Ashford,' Ann said grimly. 'She's absolutely infatuated with him. Nothing either Ralph or I say to her makes the slightest difference.'

'Calf-love,' Chelsea informed her, trying not to smile. Ralph and Ann were extremely protective of their daughter, and a high-spirited girl like Kirsty was bound to rebel. They had been the same with her. Ann, for all her placid nature, seemed to have an imagination that worked overtime when it came to the fates that could befall an unprotected girl. In Chelsea's view, Ann was almost an anachronism in this day and age; a woman who was quite content to be a stop-at-home wife and mother, and who moreover was still as deeply in love with her equally staid husband as she had been when she first met him.

'Look, I know you don't want to admit your little girl has grown up, but girls do fall madly in love at seventeen . . .'

'I'm well aware of that, Chelsea.' Ann eyed her sister frowningly. 'If it was a boy her own age, another teenager, it wouldn't matter, but Slade is far from being that. He's in his early thirties at least.'

'And Kirsty worships him from afar,' Chelsea grinned, still refusing to take her sister seriously. 'Look, love, I know Kirsty is a very pretty girl and the apple of your eye, but a man of thirty-odd isn't going to be interested in a schoolgirl.'

'You wouldn't think so,' Ann agreed, 'but he is—and interested enough to keep her out until two in the morning the other night. Ralph was furious!'

'Has he tackled him about it?' Chelsea asked frowningly. 'Does he know how young Kirsty is?'

'The situation's a very difficult one,' Ann told her. 'Slade's company has just bought out Lutons.'

Lutons Engineering was the largest firm in the small town of Melchester, and Ralph had been the Works Manager there for several years. Chelsea could quite see, without her sister needing to put it in as many words, that her gentle brother-in-law might find it rather difficult to tackle his new boss on the subject of his liaison with his young daughter. But surely the man himself must realise . . . Contempt darkened Chelsea's long-lashed blue eyes. Surely the man must know that Kirsty, for all her prettiness, was no more than a child ... a little girl still, despite her frequent attempts to appear more sophisticated—far more sophisticated than *she* had been at seventeen, Chelsea thought wryly. But then at that age she had not had the advantage of Kirsty's ripe prettiness. Well could she remember her too thin body and straight dark red hair. But at seventeen girls didn't consider themselves children. She *could* remember that.

'How about sending Kirsty off to stay with Ralph's parents for a while?' she suggested.

'Not possible, I'm afraid. Ralph's father's heart is troubling him again, and besides, I don't think Kirsty would go. She's changed, Chelsea. I barely recognise her,' Ann admitted. 'And I'm so afraid for her. Slade isn't a boy ... he's a grown man, who could never be satisfied with the sort of innocent relationship ...' Her voice trailed away and she looked helplessly at her younger sister.

'You want me to talk to Kirsty? Do you think she'd listen?'

'No. And I don't want you to talk to her exactly.' For the first time that she could remember, Chelsea saw that her sister couldn't quite meet her eyes. 'Chelsea, I hate reminding you of this' Ann began in a low voice, 'but ...'

'But if anyone can speak from experience, it has to be me,' Chelsea supplied for her in a bitter voice. 'I agree, but experience is something everyone had to learn for themselves. I know there were people enough to warn me that Darren was married, that all he wanted with me was an affair, but did I believe them? No. And I went on disbelieving them right up until I was inside the bedroom door.'

'It still hurts, doesn't it?' Ann questioned gently. 'It's nearly ten years ago now, but you've never really got over it.'

'A sensitive little plant, that's me,' Chelsea agreed with self-mockery, 'I should have listened to you in the first place. You never really wanted me to go to drama school, did you? But I insisted, and you and Ralph gave way. When Darren told me I was exactly right for the ingénue part in his new play I swallowed it completely; fool that I was. The only part he had in mind for me was the traditional role of mistress, and a very brief part at that.'

'Oh, Chelsea, don't!' Ann protested, hating to hear the bitter self-accusation in her sister's voice. 'We were as much to blame. You were far too young to leave home—we should never have let you go to London alone. When you came back that night . . .'

'My pride in tatters but my virtue intact,' Chelsea supplied dryly. 'I honestly believed that he loved me and that in time he intended to leave Belinda. He actually laughed at me when I told him that, you know—I don't know if I've ever told you that touching little detail before. Heavens, when I look back, the whole thing was more farcical than tragic, although at the time no one could have convinced me of that fact. I thought the world had come to an end, turned my back on drama school.'

'And made a first-class career for yourself . . .'

'As a repairer of ancient tapestries,' Chelsea

supplied. 'But we were talking about Kirsty, not me. What's this man like? He can't be much of a man if he needs to search the ranks of schoolgirls for female companionship.'

Ann's dry, 'Don't you believe it—he's very, very much a man,' brought Chelsea's eyes to her sister's face in astonishment. Ann pulled a face. 'Oh, it's not just that he's good-looking—and he's that all right, but he's also incredibly sexy with it. You know the type—even I went weak at the knees.'

Chelsea did. Darren had been the same, and she was beginning to dislike Slade Ashford without even meeting him.

'Well, in that case Kirsty can hardly be the only contender for his . . . attentions,' Chelsea told her sister. 'Is he married?'

'No. In a way I almost wish he was,' Ann admitted. 'Chelsea love, please, you've got to help!'

'Willingly,' she agreed, her dislike and contempt for Slade Ashford growing with everything Ann said about him, 'but how?'

'We've invited him to our anniversary party. Kirsty insisted, and of course he is Ralph's boss. You know we've decided to hold it at the Clarence?'

Chelsea nodded. The anniversary Ann spoke of was their twentieth, and she knew that her sister and brother-in-law had planned for some time to celebrate the event in some style. The Clarence was their most expensive local hotel, an old country house set in its own grounds, and the party was something Ann had been planning for for many months.

'Well, what I thought was that you ... you ...'
Ann stirred her cake mixture carefully, avoiding
Chelsea's eyes. 'I thought you could somehow get
Slade away from Kirsty,' she finished, adding
defensively, 'I know it's a cruel trick to play on
her, but kinder in the end, surely you can see that?'

'It's certainly cunning,' Chelsea agreed. 'Always
supposing it was possible. What makes you think
he'd drop Kirsty for me?'

'Haven't you looked in the mirror lately?' Ann
demanded dryly. 'Kirsty may be a pretty girl, but
you're a beautiful woman, Chelsea.'

'Well, thank you!'

'It's true,' Ann said quietly. 'You *are* beautiful,
even though you always try to deny the fact.' She
studied the rich dark red fall of her sister's water-
straight hair, and the long, dark-lashed eyes with
their sensuous, smoky darkness. A faint flush
touched her high cheekbones, emphasising the
triangular shape of her face, faintly feline and
subtly sexy, although Chelsea herself always
denied the fact. Add to that a tall slender body
with long, long legs, a narrow waist and rather
fuller than fashionable breasts, and it all added up
to a woman men looked at and looked at again.
And it was all such a waste, Ann thought
regretfully. She had lost count of the men she and
Ralph had introduced to Chelsea; the little dinner
parties they had arranged. She sighed ... Just
because she had been hurt once Chelsea seemed to
have made a decision never to let any other man
close enough to her to be hurt again.

'It takes more than physical appearance to
attract a man,' Chelsea was saying crisply. 'I'm

sorry, Ann, but it just wouldn't work. I don't have the right aura . . .'

'But you do have the right equipment, and the training to use it properly if you wanted to,' Ann reminded her quietly. 'Please, Chelsea, if you won't do it for me, do it for Ralph. He thinks the world of Kirsty. It would break his heart if she did anything . . . foolish.'

'Like letting herself be seduced by a man old enough to be her father, you mean? Are you so sure it hasn't happened already?' Chelsea asked bluntly.

Ann paled, her hands trembling slightly. 'She said it hadn't so far, but I suspect it's only a matter of time. If you could just show her that his interest is only fleeting; that he would respond to any attractive woman who made herself available to him . . .'

'So . . . I've got to make myself available to him as well as steal him away from my niece? Anything else?'

'Oh, Chelsea!' There was real anguish in Ann's voice. 'Kirsty is making a fool of herself over him. Please help! I hate having to ask you, but I can't think of anything else. I know you'll hate doing it, but with your drama training . . .'

Ann's shoulders were hunched, tears making damp tracks down her floury cheeks. Chelsea took her in her arms, remembering all the times as a child when their roles had been reversed and Ann had been the comforter.

'It's all right, love—I'll do whatever I can,' she promised. 'He must be a swine to contemplate an affair with an innocent like Kirsty. It's been a long time, though, since I was called upon to put my training into practice, let's just hope I can rise to the occasion. I seem to recall that I never was much good at the role of femme fatale!'

It was a thought that lingered in her mind on the drive back to her flat, images of Darren coming back to torment her. A stupid little prude he had called her, and worse. She had gone round to his house to read the script, or so she had thought. She had been surprised to find him dressed only in a bathrobe as although she felt herself in love with him she had been too naïve to contemplate a full-blooded affair. But she went willingly enough with him when he said his study was upstairs. She shuddered as she remembered what had followed. Darren's fury when he realised she wasn't going to give way to his advances had been a real eye-opener. He had been amused at first, and then amusement had given way to anger. Chelsea could remember quite vividly how disillusionment had warred with sickness as she listened to his furious abuse. And then his wife had returned, setting the seal on her humiliation with her amused contempt. Apparently Chelsea hadn't been the first little diversion Darren had sought. Even now, years later, her stomach heaved at the memory; because there had been a moment when because of her love for him she had been tempted to give way to him. She had loved him—or had thought she had, she thought bitterly. She had been a fool, and naïve! And now here was history almost repeating itself with poor little Kirsty!

Her phone was ringing as she entered the flat,

and when she picked it up she heard the familiar voice of her boss, Jerome Francis. He wanted to tell her about a new commission they had obtained from the National Trust. Jerome's company specialised in repairing prize tapestries and other antique fabrics, and Chelsea was his most skilled employee. She had left drama school after her débâcle with Darren, too humiliated to return, guessing that the others on the course with her must have known how Darren had been deluding her, and admitting to herself that she did not have the aptitude for the stage she had once thought. She lacked the hard, unyielding core that made a first-rate actress, one of her teachers had told her, but she had gained a certain panache; a way of moving and holding her head that drew the eye, even while she herself was unaware of it.

Instead of the stage she had turned instead to her second love, embroidery, being lucky enough to enrol at the Royal College of Embroiderers, where she had come to know Jerome and eventually to work for him.

The new commission sounded just her cup of tea. The Trust had just taken over a mansion in Northumberland. The house had been in the same family—a cadet branch of the Percys—for many centuries and had been inherited by a cousin who had decided to offer it to the Trust.

The pattern was a familiar one, but what excited Chelsea was Jerome's information that among the contents being left in the house was an extremely old tapestry, said to have been stitched by the ladies of the family during the Third Crusade.

'If everything goes well you could start work up

there when you've finished the chair covers,' Jerome suggested. 'I'll be away most of next week, so we can finalise arrangements when I get back.'

One of the joys of her job was that her work was never monotonous or boring and could and did take her all over the country, and sometimes to the châteaux and palaces of Europe, but Northumberland was somewhere she had never before visited, and Chelsea felt the familiar excitement growing in her as she replaced the receiver, her happy smile being replaced by a sudden frown as she remembered her conversation with her sister.

Ann was not a fusser, nor prone to exaggeration, and Kirsty was an enchantingly feminine girl; pretty and clever with an excellent future ahead of her, providing she did not fall into the same trap that had so cruelly mauled her, Chelsea thought grimly.

She was granted an unexpected opportunity to judge for herself exactly what danger her niece was in when she had to drive into town for some embroidery silks she had run out of.

For most of the articles she worked on, Chelsea dyed her own silks, using natural dyes of the same type as would originally have been used, and these were then cleverly faded to match the existing colours, but in this instance all she wanted was an oyster-coloured silk she knew she could obtain from a local craft shop.

Parking her car in the cobbled square which doubled as a market place on market days, Chelsea got out and walked down the narrow street which housed the craft shop, stunned as she did so to see her niece emerging from a newly opened restaurant, accompanied by a darkly tall man.

For a moment the elegance of the expensively cut charcoal grey suit, the way the lean brown fingers cupped Kirsty's elbow as they stepped off the pavement, took her back in time and she herself was seventeen again.

Fighting against anger, Chelsea stepped back automatically into the shadows, the progress of the other couple across the road affording her an uninterrupted view of her niece's escort for the first time.

One look at him and Chelsea felt her heart sink. Ann had been quite right; this man had sensuality written all over him—it was imprinted into his skin, drawn tautly over high cheekbones, olive-tinted as though he spent a considerable amount of his time in climates far warmer than Melchester's.

As he bent his head to Kirsty's Chelsea was forced to acknowledge the fascination he would undoubtedly have for a girl her niece's age—and for many considerably older.

The way he moved, his smile, the lean fitness of his body, all bespoke a maleness that would attract the majority of women.

But not her, Chelsea thought contemptuously, wishing she could forget the adoration in her niece's eyes as she looked up at him. They had now safely crossed the street and were walking past Melchester's one and only fashionable boutique when an elegant blonde emerged, the smile she gave Kirsty's escort a very clear invitation.

Chelsea didn't miss the way Slade Ashford's eyes admired the blonde's slender curves, and her fears that she wouldn't be able to free Kirsty vanished on another wave of contempt. Even when he was with her niece the creature couldn't keep his eyes off other women! What could he possibly want with Kirsty, a man of his undoubted experience? Was her very innocence the challenge which his jaded appetite demanded? Would he simply seduce her and then leave her? Not if she had anything to do with it, Chelsea vowed grimly.

She telephoned her sister when she returned home, and ascertained that Kirsty was indeed spending the afternoon with Slade Ashford.

'I didn't want to let her go,' Ann admitted, 'but what could I do? If I'd refused she'd only have arranged another meeting behind my back. I don't want to force her into lying to us.'

'Don't worry too much,' Chelsea comforted her. 'Kirsty might be blinded by adoration, but he's far from being similarly afflicted.' She told her sister briefly about the blonde. 'You know the type—skin-tight jeans, brief tee-shirt and a very come hither smile.'

'Poor Kirsty!'

'I expect he finds her refreshingly different,' Chelsea said bitterly, remembering Darren using those words about her in what now seemed another life. 'But at least it means that he shouldn't be too difficult to detach from her, and perhaps the humiliation of it being done so publicly at your party will be enough for her to refuse to see him again.'

'It ought to be,' Ann agreed. 'She shares your pride.'

'I don't think it would be a good idea to introduce me to him as your sister,' Chelsea warned Ann. 'He just might smell a rat. In fact, it might be as well if I engineered my own introduction. I suspect Kirsty will try to stick to his side like glue, so we'll have to find some means of detaching her for long enough for me to introduce myself. I only hope I haven't forgotten all my old drama training, although playing femmes fatales wasn't high on the list of our studies.'

'Perhaps not, but you're an excellent mimic,' Ann reminded her sister, 'and travelling as you do, you must have had ample opportunity to study the breed in its natural habitat.'

Chelsea grinned. If it wasn't for her concern for poor Kirsty, she might almost enjoy cutting Slade Ashford down to size. He and men like him had preyed on her sex for too long. Picturing Slade Ashford's expression when she had seen him with Kirsty, Chelsea doubted that a woman had ever said 'no' to him in his life. All the bitterness she had experienced over Darren welled up inside her. Now, she realised, she had a chance to even the score.

Like any good actress she laid her plans carefully, including a visit to London to find a suitable outfit. Something definitely provocative and sexy, she decided, as she sat in the train; something to appeal to the experienced male predator; not too blatant though . . .

She found it after several hours' search in a

small boutique tucked away off Bond Street. It was part of their new Christmas stock, the salesgirl told Chelsea as she admired it. It was also criminally expensive, but nevertheless she agreed to try it on.

Normally the rich blue taffeta dress with its tight moulded bodice wouldn't have appealed to her at all, but as she emerged from the changing cubicle to study herself full-length in the pier glass she had to admit that it suited her. The tight bodice clung seductively to her breasts, her shoulders and throat glowing softly pale against the rich fabric. The rustling skirts billowed gently from the narrow waist in piquant contrast to the sophistication of the bodice, and the salesgirl produced a matching band of velvet ribbon adorned with silk roses sewn with pearls and diamanté which she fastened round Chelsea's throat.

'If you wore your hair up very simply and just decorated with the same flowers, you'd look absolutely stunning,' she told Chelsea, scooping up her long hair to reveal the pure length of her slim throat.

The effect was a bewitching one, Chelsea admitted, and although the dress was outrageously expensive, she found herself weakly agreeing with the girl that it might have been made for her.

As indeed it might, she admitted a little later as she stepped out of the boutique, clutching a black and gold embossed box and a piece of paper on which the girl had scribbled an address where Chelsea could have a pair of shoes made up to match the dress. The boutique had also been able to provide the silk flowers to decorate her hair, and on a sudden impulse, as she was walking past the store, Chelsea hurried into Harrods and headed for the cosmetics department.

Two hours later she emerged exhausted but delighted with the new make-up she had bought in colours far stronger than those she had normally used. The salesgirls had been more than willing to show her the latest winter styles, and Chelsea had been pleased and a little startled to discover her stage training came flooding back as she memorised and elaborated in her mind, adapting what they had shown her to suit not her own personality but the image she intended to project in order to lure Slade Ashford.

The weekend before the party, Chelsea was surprised to hear someone knocking on her door and to discover Kirsty standing shivering outside in the cold east wind which was blowing.

'Come on in,' she invited her niece. 'Do you fancy a cup of tea?'

She had already noticed the storm signals flashing in Kirsty's blue eyes, and the stubborn set of her mouth, and her heart sank as Kirsty shook her head and flung herself into a chair.

'It's impossible at home,' she announced bitterly. 'Anyone would think I was seven, not seventeen!'

'Do you know,' Chelsea remarked conversationally, 'I've often noticed that people have a tendency to treat us the way we behave.'

There was a pregnant pause. She looked up and smiled guilelessly at Kirsty, adding sympathetically, 'What's wrong? Arguments over the curfew?'

'You mean Mum hasn't told you?' Kirsty asked suspiciously.

'Told me what?' Chelsea frowned. 'The last time I saw her she was full of preparations for the party.'

'I want to go to drama school,' Kirsty told her aggressively, 'but they won't let me.'

'You've still got a year to do at school,' Chelsea reminded her, her heart sinking a little. She and Kirsty had always been able to talk to one another, but here was her niece masking her involvement with Slade Ashford by pretending her quarrel with her parents was about her desire to go to drama school.

'Yes, and then I'll be eighteen; able to do exactly what I want.'

Fear shafted through Chelsea.

'The acting profession is a very gruelling and often heartbreaking one,' she warned her niece. 'You know I went to drama school?'

'Yes, but you left.'

'Not just because I realised that the stage wasn't for me,' Chelsea admitted. 'I got involved with someone I met there—an older man.' Beneath her lashes she studied Kirsty's set face. 'He was married, of course,' she continued carelessly, 'but I was far too naïve to realise that he was just using me—until it was too late. I'd hate that to happen to you, Kirsty.'

'Things are different nowadays.' Kirsty tossed her head and eyed her thoughtfully. 'I never knew you were involved with a married man.'

Chelsea winced at her choice of words.

'He was very attractive—sophisticated and extremely worldly. I thought he genuinely cared about me, but of course he didn't. How could he? We were worlds apart. I was a girl of seventeen who knew next to nothing about life, he was a man in his thirties who'd already experienced nearly everything it had to offer.'

There was a small silence and then Kirsty got to her feet.

'Mum's told you about Slade, hasn't she?' she demanded scornfully, making Chelsea wince for her own clumsiness. 'You just don't understand— any of you!'

She was gone before Chelsea could protest, black curls bouncing on her shoulders, her coltish jean-clad legs padded with scarlet striped leg-warmers a bright splash of colour as she ran quickly down the street.

Cursing herself for mishandling the situation, Chelsea paced her small living room. There had been disappointment and wariness in Kirsty's expression—and a barrier that had not been there before.

As she watched her niece disappearing Chelsea resolved that no matter what it cost she would somehow rescue Kirsty from Slade Ashford.

CHAPTER TWO

ALTHOUGH not a dedicated partygoer, Chelsea was not normally averse to accepting the many invitations that came her way; mainly as a means of in-depth study of the human

race at play. Ann often protested that she
spent far too much time watching from the
sidelines when she could have been joining in
the fun, but her experiences with Darren had
left her wary and cynical and more especially
reluctant to get involved.

Tonight, though, was different. Normally she
would have enjoyed the thought of attending
Ann's wedding anniversary gathering, but there
was no thought of enjoyment in her mind as
she made careful and thorough preparations for
the evening, the maxim of her drama school
tutors ringing warningly in her ears. 'Immerse
yourself completely in your part,' had been their
favourite command. 'Remember that when you
walk on the stage you are the character you
are playing. If the audience is to believe it,
you must believe it.' Something told her that
Slade Ashford was the most demanding 'audience' she was ever likely to meet, and so, as she
lay in a deep bath of scented water, mentally
relaxing and breathing deeply, she forced herself to
put aside her own character and assume that of
the woman who – for tonight – she was going to
be.

Her efforts were so convincing that by the time
she was ready to emerge from her bath she had
almost come to like the rich Oriental perfume she
had chosen for her role – one that normally she
would have avoided in favour of something more
Establishment.

No bra was necessary because of the way the
bodice of her dress was boned, and smoothing
fragilely sheer matching blue stockings over silkily

perfumed legs, she paused for a moment to study her appearance objectively in her bedroom mirror. Her skin was creamily pale; her breasts firm and full, the curve of her waist lending a delicate sensuality to the narrow-boned hips.

Minute petrol blue briefs matched her stockings and suspenders. Her fingertips brushed accidentally against one silk-clad thigh and with a slight grimace of distaste Chelsea turned away from the mirror. She looked like a slave girl adorning herself for the market. Unbidden, a memory struggled to be unleashed from the chains in which she had bound it—herself at seventeen, bright-eyed, eager, and more than a little embarrassed as she spent her meagre savings on cheap fake satin undies, hardly daring to imagine how she would feel if Darren saw her in them.

Fool! Fool! she goaded herself. Why remember all that tonight? And the ridiculous thing was that when Darren had tried to make love to her all she had felt was fear and revulsion. Frigid, he had called her, and with good reason.

Stop it—stop it! Her teeth ground together with her efforts to deny the memories. She had never dreamed when she went round to read the script that night that Darren would ... Somehow whenever she had envisaged them making love it had been in some secluded hideaway, remote and fairytale; not the house he shared with his wife. The moment she had realised that script-reading was the last thing he had on his mind, her desire had disappeared, too weak to overcome the suffocating awareness all around them that Darren was married to someone else.

Since then she had walked warily, too fastidious to ever allow herself to become involved with any man who had ties elsewhere and too cautious to trust even those who did not.

Her phone rang, and she went to answer it. It was Ann, ringing to bolster her courage and thank her yet again.

'Don't thank me yet,' Chelsea warned her sister. 'All I've promised to do is try.'

Half an hour later, fully dressed and made up, she studied her reflection critically. The blue dress was perfect against her pale skin and dark red hair, emphasising the rich blue of her eyes which she had deliberately emphasised with her new make-up. Gold glitter shimmered in her cleavage and along her high cheekbones. As the salesgirl had suggested, she had twisted her hair into a smooth chignon and decorated it with the blue silk flowers.

It was only when she secured the band of ribbon round her throat that her fingers betrayed a fine tremble. With their coating of lip-gloss her lips looked full and softly vulnerable, matching varnish gleaming softly on the nails she had deliberately allowed to grow. She normally detested anything other than natural or faintly pearl varnish on her nails, but tonight hers were those of a predator— dipped in blood, she thought, shuddering.

For Kirsty's sake she had to succeed, and yet already she was hating the thought of the pain she knew she would inflict upon her niece.

Rather than drive herself to the Clarendon she had ordered a taxi. It arrived promptly, and because the night was cold Chelsea pulled on a

cream wool coat which had been a present to
herself the previous Christmas.

The hotel was ablaze with lights when her taxi
drew up outside, and in the car park she glimpsed
several familiar cars. Melchester was a relatively
small market town and her family were fairly well
known. She and Ann had grown up there, and
when Ann had married the young man who had
come south from Birmingham to work for Lutons,
Ralph too had been absorbed into the closely knit
society Chelsea and Ann had known from
childhood, hence the party tonight was well
attended with the friends and families of their
school friends.

The early arrivals were clustered round the bar
of the self-contained hotel suite Ralph and Ann
had hired for the evening, when Chelsea walked in.
She left her coat with the cloakroom attendant and
quickly sought out her sister.

Apart from the slight concern shadowing her
eyes, Chelsea didn't think she had ever seen Ann
looking better; not even on her wedding day.
Maturity suited her fair prettiness, and even as
they stood side by side no stranger could have
guessed at their relationship. Ann in her early
forties was small and inclined to be slightly plump,
her fair hair cut short and waving softly round her
face.

'Chelsea!'

They kissed. Ann was wearing Guerlain's
Chamade, and raised her eyebrows slightly as they
drew apart, her murmured, 'Very, very sexy!'
drawing a reluctant smile from Chelsea.

'Where's Kirsty?' she asked.

'Oh, she refused to come with us. Apparently Slade is picking her up.' Ann sighed, and looked unhappy. 'I'm so worried about her. She's changed completely. Oh no,' she protested feelingly, 'there are the Rosses. I'll have to go and speak to them. See you later!'

Humanity the world over was much the same, separated only by the greater or lesser degree of sophistication their particular society enjoyed, Chelsea reflected, observing the delicate cut and thrust of conversation between two well-known rivals and co-members of the Town Council.

Out of the corner of her eye she noticed a slight disturbance by the door, and the suddenly prickling awareness shivering along her spine alerted her before they came into view that Kirsty and her escort had arrived.

Wondering if she was being over-sensitive in thinking how silent the room had suddenly become, Chelsea reflected that if she was successful in detaching Slade Ashford from Kirsty he would have scant chance of restoring himself to her good books. Desertion in the face of so much interested observation would be a bitter pill for any seventeen-year-old to swallow, and she was relieved to see that the son of Ann and Ralph's closest neighbours was obviously home from university. Was it really only last Christmas that Kirsty had been swooning over him? She had grown up a good deal in ten short months.

Discreetly keeping out of sight, Chelsea studied her quarry meticulously. Expensive dinner suit, obviously neither hired nor bought off the peg;

thick silk shirt; even thicker dark hair brushing the collar of his jacket. He turned, and Chelsea automatically stiffened slightly, hoping that Kirsty hadn't seen her. It was not part of her plan to be introduced to Slade Ashford as Kirsty's aunt.

Kirsty had spotted her parents. Slade Ashford cupped her elbow. Poor Kirsty, she didn't stand a chance. It was almost literally possible to see the awed reverence in the eyes of the women they walked past, as they rested appreciatively on Slade's lean form.

For almost an hour Chelsea circulated among the other guests, deliberately creating a subtle presence, a distinct awareness of her as a woman. Several men of Ralph's generation paid her heavily gallant compliments, while many of the younger ones were a little more obvious in their attentions, responding to her sensuously appealing aura.

To anyone watching her Chelsea's progress across the room had neither purpose nor pattern, but it did bring her into a circle of people barely two feet away from Kirsty and Slade Ashford. Across the room she caught Ann's eye. It had been arranged between them that when eventually Chelsea managed to get Slade's attention, Ann would distract Kirsty.

Perceiving her signal, Ann moved discreetly towards her. Summoning every ounce of control, Chelsea stepped backwards, deliberately allowing herself to collide with Slade. Her drink spilled as he turned to apologise and steady her, a cynical awareness in his eyes which at any other time would have made her writhe with shame. Out of the corner of her eye Chelsea saw that Kirsty was about to make some comment.

Clinging gracefully to Slade's arm, Chelsea bent to fuss over her shoe, which had been splashed with the contents of her now empty glass.

'Oh, what a nuisance!' she pouted.

'I think they'll dry.'

Chelsea was quite sure they would. Lifting her head slowly, she raised her lowered eyelashes and let her lips curve into a seductively promising smile. Beneath her tensed fingers Slade Ashford's arm felt like solid rock.

His eyes which she had imagined to be brown shocked her by being a deep intense jade, and as coolly mocking as her own were sensually promising.

'Oh, I'm not worried about my shoes.' The husky softness of her voice surprised even Chelsea herself. Perhaps age had turned her into a better actress than she had ever imagined—age, or perhaps necessity.

'It's my drink,' she murmured. 'I had to wait simply ages to get it—waiters never pay the slightest attention to a woman on her own, and now I've lost it.'

'Then please allow me to get you another . . .'

So far so good; she had managed to both capture his attention and very unsubtly let him know that she was alone. As she drew a rather shaky breath of relief she heard Ann saying urgently to Kirsty, 'Darling, can you spare us a moment?'

For a second Chelsea held her breath. If Slade elected to go with Kirsty there was nothing she could do about it. Her own fingertips still rested on his arm, and she could almost feel her niece's puzzled and hurt look, but she refused to yield to it.

'Quite a sweet little thing,' she said patronisingly as Ann led a reluctant Kirsty away. 'A relation of yours?'

Only she knew exactly how much satisfaction it gave her to see the slightly grim expression in those dark green eyes as Slade said curtly, 'No; the daughter of a business acquaintance—Now, your drink . . .'

Now came the most difficult part of the evening, Chelsea warned herself. She had managed to detach him from Kirsty, but now she had to keep him not only away from Kirsty for the rest of the evening, but also firmly and publicly attached to her.

She had to wait several nerve-wracking seconds before he returned to her side with a fresh Martini, and managed to draw out their mutual self-introduction for ten minutes, one half of her mind bemused and appalled by the fulsome inanities she was uttering.

'I hate coming anywhere like this alone,' she confessed when she saw his attention was beginning to waver. 'My date couldn't make it at the last moment. Oh, wouldn't you know it!' she pouted, suddenly having a brainwave as the band suddenly started playing a dreamily romantic tune. 'They would play my favourite when I don't have a partner to dance with!'

At any other time the cool irony in those green eyes would have shattered her, but tonight she was playing a part and there was no room for her normal icy reserve.

'Far be it from me to disappoint a lady,' Slade Ashford drawled, and just for a moment as he negotiated a path to the dance floor it struck Chelsea that his ironic comment could have more than one meaning, but she swiftly dismissed the thought as over-imaginative.

In keeping with the romantic mood of the evening the dance floor was dimly lit, and in the darkness Chelsea almost stumbled, shocked by the sudden warmth of Slade's fingers on her arm as he reached for her.

In his arms on the dance floor it came as a shock to realise how long it had been since a man had held her like this. She had danced, of course, but never with this intimacy, since Darren, and the hard brush of muscled male thighs against the softness of her own body as they moved in time to the music became increasingly disturbing as frissons of awareness spread upwards from her thighs. Revulsion coursed through her in waves and the need to tense her body against the alien intrusion of arrogant male flesh became over-powering, but she refused to give in to it.

Slade's hand caressed her spine, sliding upwards to stroke the vulnerable nape of her neck. Her breath caught in her throat. What chance would Kirsty have against a man like this if he chose to submit her to the full force of his sexual expertise?

She missed a step and was drawn still closer to the lean male body of her partner, her breasts crushed against the hard wall of his chest, his

breath fanning her temple. The revolving spotlight
suddenly caught them in its beam and Slade raised
his hand to the dusting of glitter along her
cheekbones, tracing it lightly. The music stopped
and she withdrew from him, smothering a gasp as
his fingers left her face to trace instead the glitter-
dusted curve of her breasts above the bodice of her
dress.

'Very enticing.' He smiled at her and in the
darkness there was no irony in his smile, and
Chelsea felt her breath catching in her throat at
the unbelievable appeal of that smile.

For the rest of the evening she clung to him like
ivy, firmly closing her mind against what she was
doing. He left her once to collect some food for
them both from the buffet tables, and Ann hurried
across to whisper,

'Keep it up—you're doing marvels! You should
have seen poor Kirsty's face when she saw you
dancing with him! She hasn't said anything, but I
suspect she's discovered that her idol most
definitely has feet of clay. Just to make sure I
thought it might be as well if she were to see you
leaving with him, if you can engineer that. He's
attractive enough for the fact that other women
are attracted to him to add a dangerous piquancy.'

Unable to do anything other than agree with her
sister's observation and worried about her niece's
reaction to her behaviour, at first Chelsea almost
missed Slade's cool, 'Do you have your own
means of transport for getting home?'

For a moment she was tempted to tell him that
she intended getting a taxi, and then she
remembered Ann's whispered suggestion, and

summoned the last of her flagging courage to say
with a slow smile,

'I'm afraid not. I was hoping someone would be
kind enough to offer me a lift.'

She couldn't have made her meaning any
plainer, and she almost shuddered to see the
cynicism carved deep in the grooves running
alongside his mouth, as he drawled, 'Allow me.'

As luck would have it Kirsty was standing with
a group of teenagers by the foyer, and as they
walked past the group Chelsea couldn't bear to
look at her niece.

At last they were out in the cool night air,
crisply autumnal with the intensely evocative and
faintly mournful scent of woodsmoke and frost
hanging in the stillness.

'Here we are.'

Slade stopped alongside a svelte, powerful-
looking car, its dark paintwork gleaming, and
paused to unlock the doors before helping Chelsea
inside. Expensive hide moulded itself to her body,
its rich smell filling the dark interior, mingling
with the tangy aftershave Slade was wearing.

'You haven't asked me for directions,' Chelsea
pointed out to him as the long bonnet nosed its
way out into the traffic.

In the darkness she could feel him glance at her,
and a nervous fluttery feeling began in the pit of
her stomach and spread outwards as he said
smoothly,

'First I thought we'd go to my place, have a cup
of coffee.'

For a moment Chelsea's brain refused to work.
When she had been planning the evening she had

never thought as far as this. Somehow she had imagined that it would end with her leaving the hotel with Slade and then getting a taxi home. She turned towards him to protest, checking as she saw the cold cynicism of his smile, and anger suddenly welled up inside her. It didn't take much imagination to guess that 'coffee' wasn't all he had in mind. The arrogance of the man! she seethed. Did he expect her to jump into bed with him simply because she had accepted a lift from him?

It wasn't purely because she had angled for a lift, honesty made her admit; she hadn't exactly kept him at a distance during the evening. Forcefully she pushed aside the thought. So Slade Ashford thought she was going to allow him to make love to her. Perhaps it was time that someone showed him that when it came to women he wasn't as overpoweringly irresistible as he seemed to think.

This thought was enough to boost her spirits and keep her doubts at bay for the fifteen minutes it took them to reach Slade's flat; one of half a dozen in a prestigious luxury two-storey block on the outskirts of the town set in the grounds of what had once been the old manor house.

With a cool economy of movement that made it impossible for her to object Slade drove the car into a garage at the back of the apartments, locked it, and escorted her into an attractive communal hallway.

'My apartment's on the second floor,' he told her, indicating the lift.

It whisked them upwards so swiftly that Chelsea felt that she had left her stomach behind. She was twenty-six, she reminded herself dryly as they emerged from its claustrophobic confines, and this wouldn't be the first time she had had to fend off unwanted advances; and it probably wouldn't be the last. Shrugging aside the tiny inner voice that warned her that Slade Ashford was different, she allowed him to usher her into a small inner hall. As he snapped on the light she had a brief impression of stunningly effective faux-marble walls in rich brown and cream, one of them mirrored to add to the illusion.

'Not my choice,' he told her, noticing her expression. 'I needed a place in a hurry and this one was vacant. I believe the previous owner was a businessman who let it to a . . . friend.' His voice was expressionless, but the meaning was plain nonetheless, and Chelsea suppressed a sudden shudder as she contemplated how narrowly she had escaped being Darren's little 'friend', his kept mistress.

'Living room's through there,' Slade told her, opening another door.

It was decorated in varying shades of pale blue and grey, with expensive silk-covered settees, and a thick pile carpet, and Chelsea wondered if it was merely her imagination which made her think that despite its luxury this wasn't a happy place.

'I'll take your coat. Make yourself at home while I get us both a drink.'

This was the moment when she should tell him that she wanted neither a drink nor his company, but he was gone before she could speak. She would tell him when he came back, she decided. Fortunately they weren't very far from her own flat, and if he refused to take her home, she could always walk. She was studying a painting when he returned, and her first intimation that she was no longer alone came when she felt his hands on her shoulders, turning her round to face him, his expression hidden from her as he bent his head and touched his lips to the soft flesh swelling above the top of her dress, following the line of gold glitter.

'Opium,' he murmured appreciatively against her skin. 'Tell me, is all of you as deliciously scented as this bit?'

'Let me go!'

The persona she had assumed fell from her like a borrowed cloak, her eyes darkening with anger and fear as she pushed ineffectively at his hard shoulders.

'Don't you think it's a little late to play hard to get?' he laughed sardonically. 'You should be honoured. I don't normally fall for such obvious ploys, but there's something about you . . .'

'I asked you to give me a lift home, not . . . not maul me!' she managed on a choked whisper.

'Maul?' His expression was ugly as he raised his head and looked at her. 'Believe me, if I really wanted to I could make what I'm doing now pale into insignificance—and don't bother starting to cry rape. There's not a court in the land that would uphold such an accusation after the way you've been putting yourself about tonight—in front of witnesses too!'

Sickness crawled through the pit of Chelsea's stomach. What was she going to do?

'Look,' she began desperately, 'there's been a mistake . . .'

'Indeed there has,' Slade agreed softly. 'I don't know what your game is—but I can make a pretty shrewd guess. However, this time you aren't getting away with it. I'm no pigeon for the plucking, and perhaps it's time that someone made you come up with the goods you're so good at offering—and then withdrawing.'

Panic clawed at her. She wanted to scream at him that he didn't understand; that she wasn't what he thought but she knew with complete certainty that he wouldn't believe her.

Impulsively she turned on her heel heading for the door, but she had barely moved a yard before she was stopped and lifted up bodily.

'Oh no,' Slade told her slowly. 'Tonight there's no running out on your obligations.'

He kicked open a door without bothering to switch on the light, and all Chelsea could see was the generous proportions of the king-size bed. She was dropped on to it without ceremony, her attempts to struggle upright suddenly ceasing as Slade closed the door and slowly started to remove his shirt. A fury she had not expected seemed to possess him.

Trapped in the sardonic gleam of his eyes, she could neither move nor think. One part of her mind registered the smooth tanned flesh of his shoulders, and the dark finely curling hair matting his chest; the play of sleek muscles as he moved and the male grace of a torso that tapered from broad shoulders into a narrow waist; while the other screamed in silent protest at the monstrosity of what was happening to her.

'What's wrong?' The soft goading words brought the colour flooding to her face. 'Don't tell me you're opting for maidenly modesty at this late stage in the game and you want me to do your undressing for you?'

Her control broke then, deep shudders wracking her body as she tried to tear her eyes from his body and failed. His hands were on his belt when she finally managed to drag her gaze away, and as he came towards her Chelsea shrank back.

She heard him swear, and then his hands were on her body, not roughly as she had anticipated, but dangerously skilful as they traced the bones of her shoulders, their path followed by his lips as he explored the vulnerability of her skin.

She started to protest, but the words were cut off by the sensual pressure of his mouth as it explored the shape of her own. Sensations she had never experienced before flooded over her. Of their own volition her lips seemed to soften and part, the sudden invasion of his mouth shocking her with conflicting emotions. One part of her longed to repudiate him; while another, hitherto un-suspected instinct urged her to yield to the sensuous pleasure he was invoking. His fingers were in her hair, freeing it from its chignon, and weaving themselves into it while he held her, making a leisurely inspection of her face with lips that teased and tantalised from her feelings she had never suspected she possessed.

Not even with Darren had she felt this dangerously seductive desire to abandon herself completely to a man's possession. Her mind was a jumble of confused thoughts as she told herself that she had been celibate for too long; that what she was experiencing was the result of repressed emotions. She gave a small moan of protest, and Slade's mouth returned immediately to hers, probing her half parted lips.

She was so engrossed in trying to rationalise the feelings she was experiencing that it was several seconds before she realised that Slade had released the zipper of her dress and was easing it slowly from her body. The knowledge froze her into shocked stillness, her instinctive impulse to conceal her bared breasts from him as the blue dress rustled to the floor, and shame washed over her as she remembered the brevity of her underwear, the sheer silk stockings and the perfume with which she had scented every inch of her skin.

Slade's, 'You certainly believe in dressing for the part, don't you?' held an unexpected contemptuous anger that burned into her, reinforced by his mocking laughter when he saw the way she had crossed her arms over her breasts.

'What the hells's that for?' he demanded grittily. 'Enticement? Don't overplay your hand; believe me, that dress you were wearing was enticement enough!'

When she didn't move but lay staring up at him in frozen horror his mockery gave way to anger, his fingers biting into her wrists as he grasped them, dragging them away from her body, no mercy in the eyes that scrutinised every centimetre of exposed flesh.

Unable to stop herself, Chelsea cringed, hating him for making her so vulnerable; for confusing her by kissing her the way he had; and now for destroying her pride and self-respect. She shuddered to think that by the time the evening was over he would know her body more intimately than she did herself, and although she had always told herself that her virginity was more accident than design, now when she was on the verge of losing it she knew that some tiny corner of her heart had never entirely given up the hope that she would give it to a man who loved her as she loved him.

'You really know all the tricks, don't you?' Slade breathed savagely. 'But feigning reluctance won't work with me. I'm not some gullible fool easily bewitched by a pair of dark blue eyes and a vulnerable mouth. But in one respect at least I'm just like any other man.' He glanced down at her body, and Chelsea felt the tension in him.

'I want you,' he said thickly, and as he raised his head she thought she saw bitter anger in the eyes which were already beginning to glaze with desire.

His hands left her wrists to cup her breasts, his eyes holding hers as his thumbs moved arousingly against the pink flesh of her nipples.

Shock gave way to fear as she felt their unmistakable betrayal, and a small moan escaped from her clenched teeth as the tormenting caress continued and Slade's lips moved tantalisingly along her throat, investigating the tremors running over her skin.

Quite when her arms slid round his neck she didn't know, but one moment, it seemed, they were at her sides and the next they were clinging to the breadth of his shoulders, exploring the male bone structure before sliding sensuously over his back.

This time when he kissed her she had no thought of holding back, the harsh rasp of his body hair against the sensitised tips of her breasts was so intensely pleasurable. She was lost— drowning in a sea of new sensations, each one more pleasurable than the last. When Slade lowered his head and trailed burning kisses against the curve of each breast fireworks seemed to explode inside her, compelling her to arch urgently against him and gasp on a wave of burning pleasure as his tongue stroked roughly against the aroused tautness of her nipples. Lost in a rainbow-coloured cloud of feeling, she dimly heard Slade's hoarse groan as he lifted his mouth from her breast and slid his hands urgently over the gentle swell of her stomach, shocking her into sudden awareness of where she was and with whom.

'Slade, no!' she protested, her desire abating as self-revulsion swamped her.

'Damn you,' he swore hoarsely, 'you can't tell me "no" now! Lord knows why when I know what you are, but I want you more than I've wanted any woman in a long time. There's something about you . . .' He shifted slightly, studying her pale outline and watching the movement of his own hand as it moved over her skin. Chelsea shivered, shocked that even now her body seemed to have a mind of its own, wantonly responding to his touch.

'Slade . . .'

The sudden shrill ring of the phone shocked her into silence. Slade swore, and for a moment she thought he intended to ignore it, but eventually he got up and left, closing the door behind him. Chelsea heard him pick up the receiver and was suddenly galvanised into action.

Her dress lay on the floor, but she ignored it. She daren't waste time. Her coat was on a chair and she pulled it on, snatching up her bag as she slid into her shoes, praying that Slade's caller would keep him occupied for long enough for her to escape. Another door led off the bedroom into an inner hall which as she had hoped opened into the marble foyer.

Her fingers trembled over the latch, made clumsy by her desperation, but at last the door was open. Not daring to slam it behind her in case the sound alerted Slade to her escape, she fled downstairs and into the cold darkness of the night.

By fortunate chance she was able to pick up a taxi just outside the apartment, and within ten minutes of leaving Slade she was inserting her key in her own front door.

Once inside she locked and barred the door, quickly stripping off everything that she had been wearing and hurrying into the bathroom, where she quickly showered, grimacing with distaste as she tried to banish from her mind her fevered response to Slade's touch.

By the time she was dried and dressed in her nightclothes she had managed to persuade herself that she had over-exaggerated her own response, and that far from experiencing pleasure in Slade's arms what she had actually felt was revulsion. How could she feel anything else when not even

Darren had been able to arouse her to desire? She stifled an hysterical laugh as she dwelled on Slade's reaction to finding that she had fled, leaving merely her dress. That dress—she shuddered. If she never saw it again she would be more than happy. Thank goodness Slade didn't know her address. He had been so determined to make her pay for the pleasure of his company that she wouldn't have put it past him to suddenly arrive at her flat, demanding that they take up where they had left off. It was ridiculous really, but just before the phone rang she had had the impression that he resented her. He had told her that he 'wanted' her, but men were notorious for their purely physical desire. Sickness welled up inside her and she raced to the bathroom, gagging suddenly as reaction set in. To think it could have been Kirsty in her place tonight! Knowing that made everything she had endured worthwhile. Her last thought as sleep claimed her was that she was glad that she would soon be going north and that there was scant chance of her ever meeting Slade Ashford again. Lutons was only one of the companies he owned, and once the takeover had been sorted out to his satisfaction Ralph was doubtful that Melchester would see very much of him. Thank goodness!

The impatient ringing of the telephone penetrated the deep layers of sleep blanketing her, and Chelsea reached muzzily for the extension phone at her bedside.

'Chelsea—thank goodness, for a moment I thought Slade must have done away with you! I've rung twice already. I thought you weren't there.'

'I'm fine, Ann,' she lied numbly. If Slade Ashford had had his way she wouldn't have been, unless it was his practice to send his women home once he had finished with them.

'Thank heavens for that!' her sister breathed. 'Ralph was furious with me for letting you leave with Slade. He told me that after the way you'd been playing up to him all night Slade might quite naturally have thought that you wanted to spend the night with him as well as the evening.'

'I'm fine,' Chelsea lied again. She had no wish to remember the black anger in Slade's eyes when he had touched her body. Disgust for her own behaviour flooded through her. She had never thought of herself as sexually repressed, 'sex-starved' to the point where she would respond physically to any experienced man—just the opposite; and yet last night . . .

'How's Kirsty?' she asked her sister, trying to obliterate Slade Ashford from her mind.

'She seems fine,' Ann told her. 'In fact she seemed more puzzled than distressed about you going off with Slade. Perhaps she's just trying to put on a brave front—I don't know, but I do know one thing—she's going out with Lance James tonight, to some disco. All we have to do now is to make sure that the rift becomes permanent. I don't suppose you . . .'

'No way,' Chelsea told her firmly. 'I've done my femme fatale bit to death—besides, I'll be leaving at the end of the week.'

'Ralph says I'm not to worry. He persists in believing that Slade was merely indulging Kirsty.

He says a man like Slade doesn't need to chase after seventeen-year-old schoolgirls, no matter how pretty they are ... Are you sure you're all right?' Ann persisted. 'You sound strange. Look, why don't you come over ...'

'Ann, I'm fine,' Chelsea interrupted firmly. With the night behind her it was easier to convince herself that she must have exaggerated her body's response to Slade's skilled lovemaking.

With a sudden start of horror she relived her flight from Slade's apartment, shuddering with distaste as she recalled the way she had been dressed. Her dress! Hysterical laughter bubbled up inside her. What was more important— the loss of a dress, or the loss of her self-respect? Besides, something told her that she would never have been able to wear it again, because at the back of her mind was the knowledge that it was tainted for her by the way she had behaved while wearing it.

For Slade Ashford it had been nothing more than simply another brief sexual encounter; an automatic male response to an available woman; a casual acceptance of a way of life which was totally alien to her.

CHAPTER THREE

IT seemed impossible to believe that she had been at Darkwater for nearly a month, Chelsea reflected, walking up the overgrown lane which led from the Dower House to Darkwater. Her task was turning out to be one of the most demanding she had ever undertaken, but instead of depressing her, the restoration work on the tapestry promised to be so potentially rewarding that even the problems it caused her were a challenge rather than a chore.

The National Trust officials who had been working on the house had now completed their work—as it had been inhabited until the death of the owner very little had needed to be done, and Chelsea knew that the Trust had high hopes of opening the house to visitors the following summer.

Because Darkwater was so remote—ten miles from the nearest border town of Jedburgh—Chelsea was staying at the Dower House. The new owner, whom Mrs Rudge the housekeeper referred to in a rather tight-lipped fashion as 'Mr Harold's newphew', was apparently away—Mrs Rudge had grudgingly informed her that he had considerable business interests which took him away a good deal.

'Not that we ever saw much of him at all before he inherited,' she had told Chelsea that morning at breakfast. 'Born and brought up in the South, he was. Mr Harold's sister married one of them stockbrokers. It would break Mr Harold's heart if he knew what was going on with the house an' all.'

'It's probably for the best,' Chelsea had told her gently, guessing that the housekeeper's feeling towards her late employer's nephew sprang from resentment at what she saw as a callous indifference to his family home. 'With death duties many families find keeping on their homes an impossible burden. At least endowing it to the Trust will ensure that it's preserved.' She knew that the Trust very rarely took on houses unless the donors were prepared to include a substantial sum of money for upkeep, which was why so many people were forced to sell their homes to developers, to be converted into flats and hotels.

Her walk took her past a newly ploughed field. Mist clung to the hedgerows as the ground dipped away; a faint riming of frost reminding her that it was less than a month to Christmas.

The red tractor in the distance executed a neat circle, its driver lifting a checked shirt-clad arm.

Chelsea waved back, her lips curving into a warm smile. The Littles, who farmed High Meadow, which had once been the home farm, had made her very welcome, especially Tom, the son of the family. Two years Chelsea's senior, he had been farming in New Zealand when his father had suffered a heart attack, and as he ruefully told Chelsea, it was sometimes hard after living one's own life to return to the parental roof.

Chelsea had found his mother to be a mine of information about the Darkwater family, although she had been surprised when Chelsea told her what she was doing in the Borders.

'Restoring a tapestry?' she had murmured. 'Well, there's a thing . . . a firescreen, is it?'

Chelsea had laughed, visualising the thirty-odd-foot length of mediaeval tapestry obviously designed to cover one of the walls in a huge baronial hall, and Mrs Little had joined in her laughter when she had explained.

Tomorrow she planned to drive into Newcastle to collect some silks she was having specially dyed. The tapestry itself, so fragile that in places it hung together on single threads, was being attached to a new backing. Once that was done Chelsea intended to clean it, using the specialised processes she had learned during her training. Old fabrics were notorious for their fragility and momentary clumsiness could ruin centuries-old articles.

As always when she saw the house she was struck by the granite hardness of it, rising out of the earth; more of a fortress than a home, its back to the sea looking down the long valley which linked England and Scotland; a formidable guardian of the Borders, and one whose owners had owed loyalty to both the English and the Scottish Crowns at various times in history.

It was hard to accept that once this green, fertile valley had run red with the blood of warring clansmen; Border reivers, a law unto themselves, too far from the civilising influences of both London and Edinburgh to heed the commands of their rulers.

Chelsea had the house to herself, and as she walked upstairs to the long gallery where she was working and where it was intended eventually to hang the tapestry she couldn't help peopling the house with those who had owned it when it was first built during the latter part of Elizabeth the First's reign. She had visited it, as she had visited so many houses on her indefatigable tours of her country, and the Trust had been given the account books detailing the family's expenditure for the occasion—and the blunt north-country statements as to the extravagance of it all.

Chelsea had always known that under her strong practical streak lurked what she considered to be a very self-indulgent tendency to daydream, but nowhere had it been given such free reign as here. Every room of the house was being restored as much as it could be to its original state at the time it had been built, although it was obvious that such modern additions as the Georgian wing designed and furnished by the Adam brothers, who had also been responsible for the Dower House, would look ridiculous furnished with wooden settles and bare floors.

As she switched on the power lamp she used to work on the tapestry she marvelled, as she did each time she saw it, that it had survived.

It had been found rolled up in one of the attics and dumped casually in the Long Gallery by one of the workmen—a chance discovery of something with the potential to rival the fabled Bayeux tapestry.

Today Chelsea was preparing the tapestry for some specialised photography. Before the tapestry had been touched, a photographic record of it had been taken, after which Chelsea and a skilled artist employed by the Trust had work unflaggingly to reproduce an accurate facsimile of how it would have looked when new, and this too had been photographed. What she would do eventually would be to compare the two and then work on the tapestry to renew it as closely as possible to what it had once been.

The phone rang as she was studying a particularly damaged piece which she thought represented a Crusader in hand-to-hand combat with one of Saladin's warriors. Frowning, she hurried to answer the phone, smiling when she heard Tom's deep, pleasant voice on the other end of the line.

'I hope I haven't interrupted you at a critical moment,' he began, 'but I wondered if you'd like to come out for a drink tonight. I could pick you up and we could go into Alnwick—in fact,' he added, 'Why don't we go this afternoon? You said you wanted to see the Percy castle. We could have a look round the town and then have dinner.'

It sounded very tempting, and Tom was quite right, she did want to see the famous Percy stronghold, guarding the road from north to south.

'What about the farm?' she demurred, not wanting to take him away from his work.

'It will survive without me for a few hours— besides, I've earned a break.'

'Then I'd love to go,' Chelsea replied promptly. In her job flexibility was a very important consideration. She had lost count of the number of times she had worked a fifteen or sixteen-hour day to complete a special job and then fallen exhausted into bed, and Jerome trusted her to work at her own pace, so she had no compunction about taking time off, knowing that before work on the tapestry was completed she would more than have made it up.

When she walked back to the Dower House at lunch time the mist had all dispersed. Breathing in the cold air appreciatively, she acknowledged that it did have a more bracing, fresher taste than she was normally used to. It would be fatally easy to fall in love with this part of the world, she admitted; she had already come to love its tranquillity and sturdy air of permanence.

Mrs Rudge accepted the news that she would be eating out that night with a shrug and a grimace. Chelsea did not take offence at her manner; she had come to know that the housekeeper's dourness was characteristic of her and not directed at Chelsea herself specifically.

The one person she did seem to actively dislike was her new employer, and Chelsea commented on this later in the afternoon when she and Tom were speeding towards Alnwick in Tom's Range Rover.

'Oh aye, she can't abide him,' Tom agreed with a grin. 'Ma will have it that it's all on account of his mother marrying a southerner.' When he saw Chelsea's expression he laughed. 'Old habits die hard up here; time was when it was unthinkable even to marry someone from an opposing clan, but that's all disappearing these days.'

Tom was a pleasant companion, full of interesting snippets of information about the countryside his family had lived in for centuries, and its inhabitants.

As they drove towards Alnwick he told her how Darkwater had originally come to be built by one of the younger sons of the Percy family, a black sheep who had come south to London to make his fortune.

'He was one of Elizabeth's handsome young men, and she eventually gave him permission to join Drake and his privateers. That was how he made his fortune. He married one of the Queen's ladies in waiting and brought her back to the Borders. Darkwater was bought and rebuilt with his profits from his buccaneering. Previously it had been owned by one of his cousins.'

'It sounds fascinating,' Chelsea told him appreciatively, 'Tell me more.'

Tom grinned, negotiating a sharp bend before saying teasingly, 'The old place has really got to you, hasn't it? Very well then, the manor was originally granted to Ranulf de Percie, by Henry the Second. His sons grew up with Henry's at court; it's even rumoured that one of them had Plantagenet blood in his veins, although that's never been confirmed. All three of them swore allegiance to Richard the First when he became king and followed him out to the Holy Land. One of them died there; another lost his life in France with Richard later, and the third returned home to marry one of his Percy cousins.'

'He must have been the one to commission the tapestry,' Chelsea murmured.

'The Black Percys, they used to be called round here,' Tom continued, 'Partially to distinguish them from their redheaded cousins, and partially for other reasons; but in all fairness I doubt they were any worse than their neighbours.'

Conversation waned as they joined the busy A-road into Alnwick, and Chelsea concentrated on the rolling countryside of the Borders, her imagination taking fire from what Tom had told her. The 'Black Percys'—the words had a sinister ring to them and, lost in the past, she felt quite a shock when Tom suddenly stopped the Range Rover.

'We're here,' he told her goodhumouredly, indicating the bulk of the Percy fortress to his right, and parked the Range Rover facing the slow-moving river flowing past them a few yards away. On the opposite side of the road a terrace of shops huddled together; an old-fashioned baker's, scenting the air with mouthwatering aromas as they left the Range Rover and walked across the busy street.

'Castle first?' Tom suggested.

It was incredible to think that this massive fortress had been built entirely by hand, Chelsea marvelled as they drew closer to the gaunt red sandstone building.

To Chelsea it was disappointing in many ways to discover that the castle had been modernised twice in its long history; once in the 1760s, in the then fashionable 'Gothick' manner, and then later in the 1850s, even down to the stone soldiers guarding the battlements, although Chelsea learned that such *trompe l'oeil* devices had been quite common in mediaeval times, mainly to puzzle and deceive enemy scouts into believing the battlements were well manned.

The views of the surrounding countryside from the towers were breathtaking, but beautiful though it was, Alnwick, or so it seemed to Chelsea, lacked much of the grimly foreboding air that made Darkwater seem the much more powerful bastion of the two.

Afterwards they explored the town's shops and paused to study the illuminated outline of the castle in the darkness of the late autumn afternoon before returning to the car to drive to the hotel where they were to dine.

There was no need for them to return to change, Tom had assured Chelsea. The hotel he had chosen served first-class food in an atmosphere geared to appreciation of the dishes rather than the patrons' clothes.

It was nearly seven when they reached it via a narrow winding country road, and Chelsea was delighted to see that the hotel incorporated what had once been one of the Border peel towers.

'Until a few years ago it was a private house,' Tom told her. 'It's been extended at the back and modernised, and they seem to do quite well from people coming up here for peace and quiet, and as I said, the restaurant has a very good reputation.'

Despite the fact that he lived at home with his parents, Tom had travelled extensively before working in New Zealand, and Chelsea found him a far more entertaining companion than many of the so-called 'sophisticated professional' men she knew in Melchester.

The hotel restaurant was attractively designed and furnished to take the most advantage of the natural, exposed stone walls and floor without in any way sacrificing either comfort or warmth. A huge open fire at one end of the room supplied the latter, and Chelsea noticed when she was handed her menu that the choice was every bit as extensive as she would have found in a London restaurant.

'I can recommend the steak,' Tom told her. 'It will be best Scotch beef.'

Heeding his advice, Chelsea gave her order. After a brief consultation with the wine waiter, Tom asked for her preference.

During the evening the restaurant gradually filled up, and although the staff were obviously busy, Chelsea found it a pleasant change not to be hurried away so that someone else could occupy their table.

Feeling pleasantly mellow, she thanked Tom for the evening as they eventually sauntered out to the car. Somehow when she was with him she found it unnecessary to adopt the defensive tactics she used with other men. Ridiculous though it sounded, in many ways he could have been the brother she had never had; a true friend whom one could depend on . . . Steady, she warned herself as he unlocked the Range Rover; you've known him less than a month . . . She glanced sideways into his pleasant, cheerful face.

'Warm enough?'

'Fine, thanks,' she assured him. 'I've really enjoyed today.'

'Me too. You know, it's a real treat to take out a girl who isn't constantly expecting compliments; who doesn't try to turn every conversation into personal channels . . .'

For the first time that she could remember Chelsea found that she was not dreading the inevitable goodnight kiss at the end of their ride with any sense of trepidation. She glanced at Tom surreptitiously. He radiated a warm steadfastness, a sturdy dependability. Her mouth quirked upwards in faint self-mockery. She was getting soft in her old age; longing for the protective caring male—but to protect her from what? she wondered soberly. That part of her nature so brutally revealed to her by Slade Ashford? Tom would never arouse her as Slade had done; she knew that instinctively and was reassured by it. Slade had reminded her too acutely of Darren and how close she had come to giving herself completely to the playwright. Deep down inside her but hitherto unacknowledged was the fear that there was vulnerability in passion, in giving oneself wholly into the keeping of another human being, and having been so vulnerable once she intended to make sure that she never was again. With Tom she would never feel vulnerable.

It had started to rain and the hypnotic sound of the windscreen wipers lulled her into drowsiness. She relaxed into her seat, leaning her head back and closing her eyes. Tom glanced at her and smiled. He had enjoyed their evening together, and hoped it would be the forerunner of many. He liked Chelsea for her honesty as much as her beauty. He was honest enough to admit that she had an untouched quality which appealed very strongly to him.

The sudden cessation of movement woke her. She opened her eyes with a start, smiling wryly as she realised that they were parked in front of the Dower House.

'How very rude of me,' she apologised, 'falling asleep like that.'

'Umm, pity you woke up when you did,' Tom grinned. 'I was rather fancying the handsome prince bit. In fact . . .' He bent towards her, his left arm curving round her shoulders, and drew her gently towards him.

There was ample opportunity for her to withdraw, but strangely enough she had no desire to do so. When he did kiss her, it was a tentative gentle kiss.

'Tom . . .'

'I know,' he said ruefully, 'it's late and you have to be up early in the morning. Me too, but I have enjoyed this evening, Chelsea, and I'd like to think there'll be others.'

His mouth was smiling, but there was a question in his eyes that couldn't be ignored.

Impulsively Chelsea nodded her head.

'Good. I suppose you'd better go in before Mrs Rudge comes out to see what we're doing.'

She paused by the front door to wave Tom off, a new buoyant mood taking hold of her. She had enjoyed the evening; they had a good deal in common, and if their relationship threatened to lack the intense sexual electricity generated by other couples, she for one did not regret the omission.

Her hand was on the door when it was jerked open from the inside, almost causing her to lose her balance.

The first thing her startled eyes encountered was a pair of male thighs encased in expensive cream gaberdine. Her glance travelled mutely upwards, and bewilderment gave way to consternation as she found herself looking into Slade Ashford's icy-cold green eyes.

'You! But . . .'

'I'm the last person you expected to see again?' he jeered. 'What do you do? Map out an area and then fish it dry?'

'You followed me up here? But . . .'

'You thought you'd covered your tracks too

well? You had,' he agreed curtly. 'I didn't come up here looking for you, but finding you is an added bonus and one of which I intend to take full advantage. You still owe me, just in case you're in danger of forgetting. I shouldn't have thought a place like this would appeal to a woman of your . . . talents.'

Chelsea's stupefaction evaporated in a wave of anger at the contempt in his voice.

'What happened?' he demanded contemptuously. 'Did you cheat on one man too many, or has it finally dawned on you that even looks like yours don't last for ever and that a doting husband is still the best form of insurance available to women like you—teasing bitches who get their kicks leading men on and then dropping them flat. Someone ought to warn young Tom about you!'

'Warn? Just who do you think you are?' Chelsea stormed at him. 'And what are you doing here?'

'I could ask the same question of you.'

'Contrary to what you seem to think, I'm here to work,' Chelsea snapped. 'I'm employed by the firm working under the National Trust up at Darkwater.'

For a moment it seemed to her that he looked surprised, but his eyes were shielded quickly by the thick dark fan of his lashes before she could be sure of what she had seen, his voice dulcet as he drawled, 'And Tom, I take it, is merely a pleasant little diversion to help while away the time?'

'He's a gentleman, which is far more than can be said for you,' Chelsea said bitterly.

'Because he says goodnight with a chaste,

adoring kiss? Oh yes, I saw it. But it didn't turn you on, did it?'

'Implying, I suppose, that your kisses did?' Chelsea flung at him, too furious for caution. 'The male ego really is incredible! You just can't believe that I might have found your touch revolting; that I might . . .'

'Merely have agreed to come back to my flat with me because you thought you were on to a good thing? Like I've just said, you still owe me, Chelsea, and I'm a man who always collects his dues.'

Just for a moment she was tempted to wrench open the door and run as far and as fast as she could, but then common sense and pride prevailed. She was not going to show fear before Slade Ashford of all men!

Fighting against the shock of his totally unexpected appearance, she marshalled her senses sufficiently to remember that while he had been insulting and questioning her, she still had no knowledge of what he was doing at the Dower House. She had just opened her mouth to demand an explanation for his presence when the door to the kitchen was suddenly opened and Mrs Rudge emerged to demand belligerently, 'So there you are, Master Slade. Yon supper's getting cold. Oh, it's you back, is it?' she sniffed when she saw Chelsea, before turning aside to mutter quite audibly under her breath about the lack of consideration of people who turned up at all hours without warning, masters of Darkwater or not.

The blood drained from Chelsea's face, her eyes

darkening to amethyst as she stared up at him.

'*You* own Darkwater?'

She didn't need his mocking assent to confirm her shocked whisper; she could read the answer in the cold green eyes and wondered dully how she had missed the proprietorial stance of the lean body, the arrogant air of ownership implicit in the hard gaze. She couldn't stay here now, knowing whose roof she was under. First thing in the morning she would have to telephone Jerome and ask to be taken off the job.

Firmly she refused to allow herself to feel disappointment that she would never complete the task of restoring the tapestry. How could she do so now? It was a job that demanded absolute concentration and dedication; she wouldn't be capable of either with Slade Ashford's presence to contend with. On a suddenly stifled breath she remembered his threat that there was still an outstanding debt between them. The tranquillity of the Borders was ruined for her now for ever; all at once it was all too easy to imagine the valley stained red with the blood of Armstrongs and Grahams.

Hardly any imagination at all was required to picture Slade Ashford riding at the head of a band of Border reivers intent on death and destruction, and perhaps even the abduction of an enemy's daughter.

It was a long time before she fell into a fitful sleep disturbed by nightmares filled with cloaked riders and the harsh sounds of warfare and burning peel towers while she herself fled despairingly on foot from the horseman pursuing her, knowing without the need to turn her head that the eyes fixed so steadily on her fleeing form would be the colour of polished jade.

CHAPTER FOUR

CHELSEA was up early, showering quickly in the bathroom off her bedroom and then dressing in serviceable jeans and a checked shirt, pulling them on with brisk determined movements.

As she stepped out of her room the door opposite opened and Slade Ashford stood there, a towel draped round his neck, his body bare to the waist. Her breath caught in her throat as she looked away hurriedly, her face burning from his openly sexual exploration of her slim jeans-clad frame.

'Tell Mrs Rudge to hurry up with my tea, will you?' he demanded carelessly.

It was unnecessary for her to pass on the message, because she bumped into the housekeeper in the hall. Mrs Rudge's mouth was compressed into grim disapproval, as she muttered, 'The old master wouldna ha' tolerated none of this. You'll find your breakfast in the dining room,' she told Chelsea. 'Coming and going without a word of warning . . . inconsiderate, that's what he is!'

Her brother-in-law had mentioned that Slade Ashford had widespread business interests, and Chelsea wondered how frequent his trips north were.

Unable to face any breakfast, she hurried

straight to the study and picked up the phone, quickly dialling Jerome's home number.

He answered almost straight away, sharp anxiety giving way to pleasure as he heard Chelsea's voice.

'Don't you dare tell me *you're* not feeling well!' he warned her before Chelsea could speak. 'Louise has just been rushed into hospital with acute appendicitis.'

Louise was the only other skilled embroiderer he employed, and Chelsea's heart sank. She had been hoping to persuade him to allow her to swop jobs with Louise, but in the present circumstances she could scarcely do so now. Louise's job was nearly complete, and Chelsea knew that the National Trust were anxious to have work on the tapestry completed as quickly as possible.

'Chelsea, *are* you all right?'

'I'm fine,' she lied. 'I was just ringing to tell you that the tapestry is coming on very well.'

'Thank goodness for that! I badly needed some news.'

They chatted for a few minutes and Chelsea was just hanging up when a soft footfall made her spin round, the receiver clutched in one hand as she glared angrily up at the tall male figure lounging against the closed door, hands thrust into the pockets of his jeans emphasising the powerful muscles of his thighs.

'Another string to your bow?' Slade drawled. 'Does your employer know you make personal phone calls during his time?'

'That *was* my employer,' Chelsea gritted at him, 'and for your information, I was ringing him to ask if I could be taken off this job.'

'Why? Scared I'll blow your cover?'

Anger flooded moltenly through her veins.

'Nothing you could do could frighten me,' she told him furiously.

'No? Then perhaps it's time it did.'

Before she could stop him he had crossed the room, grasping her wrist with one hand while the other removed the telephone receiver. Before she had time to react she was trapped between Slade and the desk. Fear coursed through her at the proximity of his body; her own acutely sensitive to the heat coming off it; the dark hairs sprinkling arms bare to the elbow where he had rolled up his shirt sleeves. A muscle beat in his jaw, and she realised that his eyes were not, as she had thought, completely green, but flecked with yellow like those of a jungle animal, holding her in thrall.

'No!'

The sharp denial rang out between them, then the electric silence was suddenly broken as the telephone rang shrilly.

'This I believe is where we came in,' Slade drawled sardonically as he released her and reached for the receiver. 'But it isn't over between us yet by a long way, Chelsea.'

Her legs were shaking as she stumbled out of the study. Mrs Rudge was waiting outside, so close to the door that Chelsea was sure she had been eavesdropping.

'Gallivanting off again he'll be now, no doubt,' she commented, sniffing disapprovingly. 'The master should have married and got himself some sons.'

Sentiments with which she was totally in accord, Chelsea reflected bitterly as she forced down a piece of toast and drank her coffee scalding hot in her haste to be gone from the table before Slade reappeared.

Where before she had loved the remoteness of Darkwater, now she wished it was closer to the village and that it was possible for her to find accommodation there, but she knew that it was impossible. For one thing she hadn't brought her car north with her, and for another she already knew that there was no hotel or efficient public transport service from the village to Darkwater. Like it or not, she was forced to accept Slade Ashford's hospitality until her work was completed.

And the annoying thing was that there was no way the work could be rushed without risk.

There had been an overnight frost that made a lacy wonderland from dead bracken and grasses. A rabbit scampered away as Chelsea walked down the drive, a plover hung against the autumn blue of the sky. Gradually as she walked her anger started to drain away, and her mouth began to twitch slightly as she started to appreciate the macabre humour of the situation. Slade Ashford must have been as shocked as she had been herself!

She bit her lip, suddenly remembering his arrogant claim that all was not at an end between them. She had sensed on the night of the party that he was not a man to make a fool of lightly, but she had told herself that no harm had been done, and none would have been if their paths hadn't chanced to cross again like this.

For a moment she toyed with the idea of telling him the truth, but dismissed the idea as too dangerous. She had no guarantee if she did that he would not simply return to Melchester and savagely undermine all that she and Ann had done.

No, there was simply no other course open to her but to carry on as though nothing had happened and hope that given time he would either tire of seeking retribution or come to see that he had been mistaken in her.

The phone rang while she was busily engaged in checking the dyed embroidery silks which had been delivered that morning.

It was Tom on the line, and Chelsea acknowledged with a pang of remorse that Slade Ashford's presence had almost driven Tom from her mind.

'Just wanted to thank you for last night,' Tom told her cheerfully, 'and to coax you into coming out to dinner with me again tonight—some friends of mine are having a dinner party.'

'I'd love to,' Chelsea told him warmly. Going out with Tom would mean that she wouldn't be forced to spend an evening in Slade Ashford's company.

When he had hung up her work engrossed her, and studying the faded design of stitched figures under a strong lamp and a magnifying glass she forgot everything in the wonder of the story stitched by so many busy female fingers so very long ago.

Slade Ashford would have fitted better into those times than the 1980s, she thought wrathfully at one point. He was the archetypal macho male with firmly entrenched views about women's inferiority; their lack of any right to the same sexual freedom he so clearly and arrogantly demanded for himself.

Busily feeding her growing anger, Chelsea ignored temporarily her own view that women who indulged in sex purely for sex's sake were a very rare breed indeed and that unlike men most women were vulnerable through the emotional commitment they gave automatically and sometimes unknowingly whenever they gave their bodies.

When the growing darkness made further work on the tapestry itself impossible Chelsea returned to the photographs and drawings, working out in her own mind her next task, and feeling a tiny thrill of pride as she studied the work she had already done.

'How demure—and how deceptive!'

She dropped the tapestry and spun round, feeling at a disadvantage in her kneeling position, as her eyes slid upwards over long, lean legs encased in jeans.

'Coming to check up on me?' she asked sweetly.

'Your employer and I obviously see you in differing lights,' Slade told her. 'The letter passed on to me from the National Trust described you in the most glowing terms, otherwise you would not be staying in my home . . .'

'Your home?' Chelsea raised her eyebrows. 'According to Mrs Rudge until you inherited you barely visited the place.'

He shrugged, patently unconcerned by the housekeeper's criticism. 'She doesn't approve of me, or rather the fact that my father came from the south, but in point of fact she's quite wrong. I used to spend a fortnight with my uncle every year while she was away. Perhaps my northern blood is stronger than the southern, I don't know, but certainly I feel more at home up here . . . more in tune with my surroundings.'

'I'll bet,' Chelsea muttered under her breath. 'Rape and pillage would be just your style!'

'We considered it taking back what was rightfully ours and righting old wrongs,' he countered smoothly, making alarm tingle over her skin as she remembered his claim that she still owed him an outstanding debt.

His abrupt, 'Have you finished here for today? Mrs Rudge tells me that you normally get back about five,' caught her off guard.

'I can't work once the daylight fades,' Chelsea defended herself, thinking he was making a crack at lack of application to her job. 'And I don't take a lunch hour.'

'Neither, it seems, do you possess a powerful torch,' he frowned. 'You shouldn't be walking out there alone.'

'Who's going to hurt me?' Chelsea scoffed. 'A stray sheep—or perhaps you're thinking of the ghosts of your rebellious ancestors?'

'What I'm thinking of are the dangers of all too alive poachers and vagrants. We've already had problems once during the summer with a bunch of skinheads and their girl-friends who wanted to take up residence at Darkwater.' He saw her shiver and smiled grimly. 'Quite . . . From now on I'll arrange for you to have transport. There's a car in the garage that used to belong to my uncle, while you're up here you'll use it. Understood?'

'You're too kind.'

'Very probably,' came the dry response, 'but rape and violence aren't made more palatable simply because the victim is a sexual tease. Tonight I'll walk back to the house with you myself.'

The temperature had dropped several degrees while Chelsea had been working and she was glad of her thick hooded jacket when they stepped out into the darkness of the lane. A cold east wind seemed to cut right through her, and she stifled a small start of surprise when she suddenly found Slade Ashford standing between her and the icy blast which had set her shivering. As they walked down the lane he made no move to guide or touch her, which for some obscure reason increased her tension. He was only a man, she reminded herself; no different from any of the others she had known. And yet he was different. For one thing, he was the only man who had ever penetrated the barriers she had erected around herself after Darren. She shuddered suddenly; not because of the wind, but because of the memories suddenly evoked; the response of her own body to those lean knowing hands.

'Cold? We'll soon be there. They're forecasting snow in the wake of this cold spell.'

As they walked he talked about the area and his family's connection with it, which might have disarmed someone else, but to Chelsea his very urbanity only served to deepen her distrust of him. She didn't deceive herself that this was anything other than a brief armed truce between battles. When she had walked out on him she had hurt his pride, and he was a man who, she sensed instinctively, would go to tremendous lengths to assuage such a hurt.

The moment they entered the house Mrs Rudge pounced on Slade, relaying a string of messages, giving Chelsea a chance to escape to her own room, where she stayed until Mrs Rudge came up with a tray of tea and an envelope addressed in Ann's sloping handwriting.

Chelsea read it quickly. Kirsty, it seemed, had fully recovered from her infatuation for Slade, although Ann said that she had deliberately not talked to her about it. She was still as keen as ever to go to drama school, but was now also showing signs of willingness to do a secretarial course—a result of her growing friendship with Lance James, Ann wrote.

In her last paragraph Ann's handwriting suddenly tensed a little as she wrote that Ralph had just told her that Slade was leaving Melchester to return to his home in the Borders. 'I shall keep my fingers crossed that you don't run into him,' she had written, 'although Ralph says I'm being over-pessimistic in fearing you might. We don't know his home address, but Ralph tells me he's only spending a few days there before flying out to New York to spend Christmas with friends.'

When she finally put the letter aside Chelsea's tea had grown cold, and her lips formed a rather wry smile. Ann would have kittens if she wrote back and told her the truth! But at least the letter had contained some good news. She now knew that Slade wouldn't be staying at Darkwater for very long.

All she had to do was to keep out of his way during his brief stay in the Borders. For all his threats she didn't believe he was the type of man who would physically force himself upon a woman who didn't want him. She grimaced slightly, admitting that he was the sort of man women ran to, not from; she wasn't going to make the mistake of underestimating him. He would use subtle weapons in the war he had declared between them. She had a brief but illuminating memory of how her body had betrayed her in his arms, and suspected that he remembered it too, and intended to use it against her. But he wouldn't get the chance. What had happened that night had been the result of many differing factors, and he would not find her so off guard again.

As she dressed for her date with Tom, Chelsea banished Slade Ashford firmly from her thoughts.

A dinner party, Tom had said, and she glanced thoughtfully through the small wardrobe she had brought with her, working clothes in the main—jeans, jumpers, shirts, and an almost severely cut plain black dress in fine wool crêpe with a high, boat-shaped neckline and a straight skirt embellished with a fan of pleats at the front. It was nothing like the dress she had worn for her sister's party, and far more in accord with her own tastes.

She applied her make-up with care and subtlety, standing back after she had darkened her eyelashes with mascara to study the finished effect. Skilfully shadowed dark blue eyes stared half mysteriously back at her, blusher emphasising the shape of her face. Against the matt blackness of her dress her skin glowed like porcelain. A gold belt cinched round the slenderness of her waist added a party touch, as did the gold orchid earrings which had been a Christmas present from Ralph and Ann the previous year; her hair was a dark red waterfall of silk that rippled as she moved.

Tom as usual was prompt. Chelsea was just descending the stairs when she heard him drive up. When he rang the bell there was no sign of Slade, much to Chelsea's relief. Mrs Rudge let Tom in, and a broad grin creased his face as he stared up to where she had halted on the stairs. The only coat she had with her was the cream wool hooded jacket she had worn earlier in the day, but she was glad of it when she stepped outside. If anything it had grown colder. The older and more experienced farm workers were forecasting a hard winter, Tom told her as he settled her comfortably and opened his own door. The hedges were already stripped of berries, always a warning sign, and they might even have snow for Christmas.

Would she be going home? he asked as they drove down to the main road.

Chelsea shook her head. In view of the events of Ann's anniversary party she had decided against spending Christmas with her sister and her family this year, as she normally did. It might be the last that Kirsty would spend at home, and she didn't want to spoil it for them by reminding her niece of Slade's perfidy. Did he ever spare a thought for her niece, Chelsea wondered, or was she just a briefly entertaining interlude now forgotten?

'Then you must come to us for Christmas Day,'

Tom told her. 'Mrs Rudge normally goes to Jedburgh to spend Christmas with her sister, and I can't think of anything worse than spending Christmas Day alone.'

'It's very kind of you,' Chelsea thanked him, 'but I'm sure your parents won't want a stranger in their midst.'

Tom grinned. 'You don't know northerners! They might seem dour and reserved, but inwardly ... You'll have to be prepared for a grilling, though. Ma normally invites the whole clan round and they'll all be wanting to get a good look at this southern lass who's been going out with "our Tom"!'

Sharing his laughter, Chelsea reflected again how much she liked Tom. And yet despite his flippancy she sensed that underneath, despite having travelled widely, at heart he was as conservative as his parents and would make much the same sort of husband and father as his father and grandfather had done before him; steady, reliable, hard-working, allowing his emotions to show only rarely and then in private. To his wife he would give his love and loyalty and in response would expect the same from her—a tempting prospect.

She was unaware that she had sighed until Tom's hand left the wheel to touch her arm lightly.

'You don't have to come, you know. I just thought . . .'

Her thoughts had travelled so far from Tom's invitation for Christmas that it was several seconds before she realised what he meant.

'Oh, it's not that,' she assured him. 'But

actually I had intended to work over Christmas. The Trust want to get the house finished as quickly as possible because they want to open it to the public next summer. These houses are so expensive to run that every penny of revenue is needed.'

'Umm. But Slade Ashford's been pretty generous in that respect, from what I hear. Of course he's virtually a millionaire, so I daresay he won't miss it. He inherited several engineering firms from his father, and has since added to them, and then old man Percy wasn't exactly short of money, although you'd never have known it. "Close", we call it up here.'

Chelsea wasn't surprised to learn the extent of Slade's wealth. It showed in the panache with which he reacted to life; the cool arrogance overlaid with a superficial charm which did little to conceal the sheer grit of the personality beneath. Experience told her that no man was as financially successful as that without the qualities of strength and determination—and the ability to be ruthless when necessary. The knowledge did little to lessen her conviction that she had made for herself a dangerous adversary, but she comforted herself with the thought that there was little he could accomplish in the short time before now and Christmas, and by the time he returned she hoped her task would be complete. Like Darren, she suspected, he was planning a careful campaign, designed to bring her voluntarily into his arms, but what he didn't know was that her reaction to him that night was never likely to be repeated and that there was no force on earth that would bring her willingly into such close physical proximity to him again.

'Here we are.' Tom parked the car deftly in front of the small Victorian house several miles out of the village. It belonged to the local doctor and his wife, who were apparently close friends of his. 'Val and I were at school together,' he explained as he helped Chelsea out of the Range Rover. 'You could have knocked me down with a feather when she married Guy. He'd been in private practice in London,' he told Chelsea. 'His first wife was killed in a car accident and he moved up here with Sandy—that's his daughter. She's training to be a doctor herself now, but she's at home at the moment.'

As Chelsea had expected from Tom's brief comments, Valerie Charnley was some fifteen years younger than her husband, a tall fair-haired man with shrewd eyes and a wry smile. Valerie in direct contrast was small and dark with a bubbling personality and a friendliness that put Chelsea at her ease immediately.

'No wonder Tom's been keeping you under wraps,' she grinned as she took Chelsea's coat. 'He's a canny lad, is our Tom—Guy, be a darling and pour them a glass of sherry, while I go and check on the kitchen, will you?' she appealed to her husband. 'You'd never believe that I once coped quite efficiently running my own business, would you?' she grimaced to Chelsea, 'but somehow since the arrival of my twin terrors six months ago I seem to be losing my grip.'

'Take no notice of her,' a new voice chimed in. 'She's always running herself down. And before you ask, my bellicose young half-brothers are both fast asleep.'

'Thanks, Sandy, you're an angel!'

There couldn't have been more than half a dozen years' difference in the ages of the two women, but Chelsea sensed that Valerie and Sandy had an excellent relationship, which seemed all the more surprising when one reflected that Sandy must have been a teenager when Valerie married her father.

Her own offer of help in the kitchen was firmly refused, and while Tom and their host talked about the probability of snow before Christmas Chelsea explained to Sandy what she was doing at Darkwater House.

'I love the Borders,' the younger girl told her. 'Which is quite strange really, when you think that until we moved up here I'd never been north of Watford. My mother adored London.' Her eyes rested momentarily on her father. 'And moving up here was certainly the best thing for my father. It's marvellous to see him with Valerie and the twins. I'm hoping to go into practice with him when I qualify. Is it serious between you and Tom?'

The abrupt change of front surprised Chelsea.

'We barely know one another,' she told her. 'I've only known him a few weeks.'

'Sometimes it only takes minutes to feel you've known someone all your life.'

The door bell rang, and Sandy excused herself to answer it. Chelsea heard the door open and then sounds of laughter in the hall.

A frisson of awareness ran over her, her heart dropping as the door opened and Sandy returned, accompanied by Slade Ashford.

Valerie emerged from the kitchen, flushed and smiling with pleasure as she accepted his kiss.

'Slade! Mm, you smell lovely, you gorgeous creature. What a pity I'm an old married lady.'

Everyone apart from Chelsea laughed. She went through the motions, but she felt as though her cheekbones were set in cement. Watching Valerie in Slade's arms she had experienced an acute sense of . . . of what, she asked herself, trying to analyse the feeling that had overwhelmed her, suddenly glad of Tom's comforting arm along her shoulders, and the protective bulk of his body next to her.

She wasn't surprised to witness Slade conducting a light teasing flirtation with Sandy across the dinner table, but what did surprise her was Guy's tolerant acceptance of it. Sandy was only a couple of years older than Kirsty, and although she was obviously more worldly-wise Chelsea suspected that at heart she was as inexperienced as her niece. Once or twice she thought she saw Tom frowning, and found it odd that he should be concerned for Sandy when their host obviously wasn't.

As for Sandy herself, there could be no mistaking the flush on the younger girl's face, or the light in her eyes as she responded to Slade's comments.

Chelsea was dismayed to see how her hand trembled as she reached for her wine glass, and quickly withdrew it. What on earth was the matter with her? It was no affair of hers if Slade flirted with Sandy. A taste for young inexperienced girls was obviously something else he shared with Darren, she thought distastefully. What was it about innocence that made men like him want to destroy it? An insatiable ego that led them to use all the formidable weaponry at their command; all the charm and sensual expertise gained, although their silly innocent victims never realised it, in the seduction of their predecessors; in the pursuit and eventual destruction of their prey. With consummate skill they stalked and controlled the hunt until their quarry, blinded by adoration and 'love', offered themselves as willing victims on the altar of a warped male ego.

Watching Sandy was like seeing herself as she had been with Darren. An almost physical sickness rose up inside her and she could barely touch her food.

They had just finished their dessert when the telephone rang. Guy excused himself to answer it, and came back, smiling slightly. 'Not for me this time,' he told Tom, 'although the crisis is familiar. One of your cows has gone into premature labour. They've rung for the vet, but your mother thought you'd want to know.'

'Yes. I'm afraid we'll have to leave,' Tom told Chelsea. 'Bluebell's had problems before and I ought to be there . . .'

'There's no problem, Tom,' Slade told him easily, standing up, 'Chelsea can come back with me. It will save you time.'

Indecision was written plainly on Tom's face. Chelsea sensed his anxiety to get home and silently cursed the fates which had decreed that Bluebell should start to calve on this of all evenings.

'Yes, you must go, Tom,' she agreed quietly, not looking at Slade.

'I'll give you a ring in the morning. Sorry about this, everyone,' he apologised, kissing Valerie's cheek and rumpling Sandy's straw-blonde hair as he walked past. 'Pity you're training to be a doctor and not a vet,' he teased. 'Tonight you could have got some practical experience.'

'Huh,' Sandy retorted, 'as though you'd let a mere woman near one of your precious cows—I know you, Tom Little!'

A little to Chelsea's surprise it was Sandy and not Valerie who accompanied Tom to the door, and when she returned the young girl looked at her so searchingly that Chelsea wondered if she suspected her of trying to flirt with Slade in her absence—it was that sort of look, and she longed to reassure her that she had no interest whatsoever in him.

It was just after eleven when they eventually left. The wind had dropped but it was bitterly cold, and Chelsea shivered in her thick coat as she waited for Slade to start the Ferrari's engine.

The Ferrari gave a much smoother ride than Tom's Range Rover, until they came to the rutted lane leading to the Dower House. A sudden pothole in the road threw Chelsea against the broad dark-clothed shoulder next to her as the sudden jolt caught her unawares. Slade's right hand left the wheel to steady her, his fingers biting into her flesh.

'Sorry,' she apologised curtly, hating the mocking glance he gave her. Did he think she had deliberately fallen against him?

'No need to apologise,' he drawled. 'This road is appalling. I must get something done about it—

either that or get myself a Land Rover, but there's not much point in doing anything now until the winter's over. The combination of salt and ice is lethal on freshly laid tarmac, but the Ferrari certainly isn't built for this sort of terrain.'

'A city dweller, like its owner,' Chelsea suggested sweetly.

Slade brought the car to a halt in front of the house and she froze suddenly in her seat.

'Waiting for something?'

In the darkness her face flushed anger, making her tremble as she reached for the door handle. Was he trying to imply that she had expected him to make love to her?

With false sweetness she said softly, 'Forgive me, for a moment—I forgot that you weren't Tom.' Triumph glittered in her eyes as she added, 'He always opens the door for me.'

She almost had it open when Slade leaned across, imprisoning her against her seat with his body. Neither of them was deceiving the other, and she knew the taunt about Tom, which had had nothing to do with the car door, would not go unpunished. It didn't.

Slade was looking at her in a way that was unmistakable even in the semi-darkness. His left hand reached for the door handle, his arm imprisoning her. The door swung open and his arm was slowly withdrawn, brushing with subtle menace against her breasts. She was shaking from head to foot when she emerged from the car. The impulse to run into the house was overpowering, but somehow she mastered it. Behind her she heard the Ferrari engine fire, and despite the cold perspiration broke out on her forehead. On unsteady feet she headed for the kitchen, longing suddenly for a cold drink to steady her.

She let the tap run and found a glass. She was just filling it when she heard the door open. She drank the ice cold water quickly.

'Going somewhere?'

Slade's voice was almost as icy as the water had been, and Chelsea felt herself shiver. She felt him move behind her, stiffening when he gripped her shoulders, the hard touch of his fingers burning through her dress.

'Let go of me!'

His only response was the subtle alteration in his touch from imprisoning to sensual caressing as his thumbs moved rhythmically over the tense muscles of her shoulders. His left hand gathered up the fall of her hair, his thumb moving sensually over the exposed vulnerability of her nape. Rigid with anger, she breathed in sharply, clenching every muscle against him. For all the impression it made she might just as well have not bothered. Effectively imprisoned between his body and the kitchen units, she had no means of escape when his head lowered and his mouth moved slowly over her neck, brushing it lightly, bringing her out in goosebumps as she tried not to react. The light, almost teasing kisses continued. She felt his hand on her zip, his lips tracing the exposed line of her spine before returning to the smooth curve of the neck, and icy shivers alternated with a hot dryness that enveloped her skin. Outrage warred with a heated upsurge of physical response, as Slade's lips continued to nibble provocatively at her skin. It took every ounce of willpower to resist the fierce tug of desire surging through her; to suppress the small startled sounds of pleasure threatening to betray her as his mouth continued its damaging assault on her defences. She closed her eyes to strengthen her resolve, but it was a fatal mistake. Without the mundaneness of their surroundings to concentrate upon she was lost in a black velvety darkness which intensified a thousand times the pleasurable sensation of Slade's mouth moving gently over her skin, seeming to know instinctively just where to linger. A small sound of pleasure escaped her compressed lips, and as though it were the sign he had been waiting for Slade turned her into his arms, sweeping aside the dark fall of her hair and exerting just enough pressure on her neck to fully expose the vulnerability of her throat to his mouth.

Pleasure washed over in surging waves, and her head fell back against his shoulder as his lips plundered the pale flesh of her throat and shoulders, moving seductively against them until she was groaning huskily with pleasure, her fingers entwined in the thick darkness of his hair, everything but the sensations he was arousing within her forgotten.

His free hand covered the place where her heart thudded shallowly against her skin, moving upwards to stroke sensuously over her breast.

A fierce heat engulfed her. When he reached for her zip she made no attempt to stop him. Suddenly Slade froze, and then calmly zipped up her dress and released her, switching on the kitchen light and reaching past her for the kettle.

Chelsea's senses reeled, and her own movements were sluggish and apathetic. She felt as though she had been caught up in an alien force against which she had no defences. Her body felt weak and she was trembling.

Damn him she thought bitterly watching him fill the kettle. He had done it again! She opened her mouth to tell him how much she detested him, but he forestalled her, smiling mockingly as he murmured softly, 'Save it . . . Mrs Rudge is on her way down, and you wouldn't want her to get the wrong idea, would you?'

Her eyes rounded with disbelief and then she heard the unmistakable sounds of the house-keeper's imminent arrival. Humiliation writhed through her. When she had been lost to everything but the feelings he had aroused he had been sufficiently detached to hear the housekeeper moving about. Something seemed to have gone badly wrong. It was men who were supposed to be so vulnerable to passion that they forgot everything else, wasn't it?

Passion! A bitter smile touched her lips as she used the housekeeper's entrance to make good her escape. Much more of this and he would have her believing that she was suffering from a frustration so acute that his touch was enough to bring it surging to life.

CHAPTER FIVE

In the morning there was no sign of Slade, and Mrs Rudge told Chelsea acidly that he had had to go into Newcastle on business.

She was just on the point of leaving the house when the housekeeper suddenly produced a set of car keys which she handed begrudgingly to Chelsea, watching her speculatively.

'Told me to give these to you and said you were to make sure you used the car. Out driving it, he was this morning before he left.'

For a moment Chelsea was tempted to tell Mrs Rudge in no uncertain terms that she had no intention of using the car, but caution prevailed. She had no intention of arousing the woman's curiosity even further, and it had occurred to her that with the car she might be able to find alternative accommodation.

With this in mind she drove up to the farm shortly after three o'clock, intending to ask Tom's mother if she could recommend somewhere where she could stay.

She found Mrs Little in the large old-fashioned farmhouse kitchen. The appetising smell of newly baked bread filled the stone-flagged kitchen, and Chelsea sniffed appreciatively as she followed Mrs Little inside.

'Fancy a slice, do you? It will give you indigestion, mind,' she warned, chuckling at

Chelsea's obvious battle against temptation.

'Tom isn't here,' she told Chelsea several minutes later when they were both sitting down at the scrubbed wooden table. 'He had to go into Jedburgh.'

'It's not him I've come to see,' and Chelsea quickly explained the purpose of her visit.

'Hmm. Finding a room hereabouts won't be easy. There's none to be had in the village, that I know of. Not making you comfortable at the Dower House? Janet Rudge is a sour old besom right enough . . .'

'It's got nothing to do with Mrs Rudge,' Chelsea told her hastily, avoiding her eyes as she added, 'It's just that now that Mr Ashford has returned, I thought he might want his home to himself.'

She purposefully avoided Mrs Little's shrewd eyes as she added the last remark, but felt that she had not totally deceived her when the older woman mused thoughtfully,

'Aye, well, there's them as would be pretty quick to jump to the wrong conclusions if Janet Rudge wasn't living there, and young Slade's a fine-looking man; takes after his mother's family for his looks. I mind well his uncle when he was his age. A bonny lad he was, with all the lasses wild for him. I'm sorry, lass,' she apologised when Chelsea remained silent, 'but if it's lodgings you're wanting I doubt that you'll find anything local.'

The kitchen door swung open as she spoke and Tom strode in, patently surprised and pleased to see Chelsea there.

'Sorry about last night,' he apologised, when she

had explained the purpose of her visit, and he had agreed with his mother about the unlikelihood of her finding alternative accommodation, 'but at least you had Slade to take you home.'

'Yes.' Chelsea forced a noncommittal smile and glanced at her watch. 'Heavens—I'd better be going. I'd no idea it was that time.'

'I see Slade's fixed you up with your own transport,' Tom commented. 'If you've got a minute I'll show you the new arrival who interrupted our dinner party.'

The calf was penned into a stall with her mother, and Chelsea marvelled at the tiny huge-eyed creature as she watched it suckle greedily.

'Everything obviously went all right, then,' she observed as he walked her back to the car.

'It was touch and go for a while, but in the end it wasn't as bad as we feared—which reminds me, I've still got to make my apologies to Val. Could you drop me off in the village? The Range Rover's down there having new tyres fitted ready for the snow they're forecasting. I can pick it up and make my apologies at the same time.'

Chelsea had to suppress a small grin as she watched Tom folding his large frame into the small front seat of the car.

She was a competent driver and was pleased to see that Tom had no obvious bias against female drivers. It took them a little over thirty minutes to reach the village. Tom directed her to park in a quiet side street off the main road and several yards from the garage.

'Why down here?' she asked him, puzzled, glancing through the back window towards the main road. 'I could have dropped you off outside the garage.'

'I know, but if you had I wouldn't have been able to do this,' Tom said softly.

His kiss took her by surprise. The pressure of his mouth was warm and firm with no hint of the steel male dominance she had experienced with Slade. Refusing to admit even to herself that pleasurable though the brief embrace had been it in no way stirred her blood as Slade's had done, Chelsea murmured protestingly in Tom's arms.

A dark car flashed past and he released her reluctantly. 'I'm afraid the setting's not as romantic as it would have been last night,' he apologised ruefully. 'I'll give you a ring later in the week. Perhaps we can arrange to go out together?'

As she watched him stride down the street Chelsea sighed. She liked Tom very much, but she had the feeling that he was rushing her, and it made her wary. After Darren she had vowed that no man would ever get close enough to her emotionally to treat her as he had done—and yet here she was breaking that vow twice over. Shivering a little, she re-started the car and drove slowly back towards the Dower House.

She parked the car carefully in front of the house and then let herself in with the key Mrs Rudge had given her. The first thing she saw was a note on the hall table from the housekeeper saying that she had gone down to the village to do the flowers for the church.

Chelsea knew that Mrs Rudge was one of a small group of ladies responsible for decorating the small Norman church in the village, and normally on these occasions the housekeeper was absent for several hours, spending the evening with a friend who collected her in her car and then brought her back again.

She would just make herself a light omelette for her supper, she decided, making her way upstairs. She felt tired and was unwilling to admit that she was finding it hard to deal with the physical presence of Slade Ashford in the same house. Like water constantly dropping on a stone, his acerbic comments and mocking glances were wearing away her self-possession, making it harder and harder for her to assume a mask of indifference towards him.

Even without the added complication of what had happened at Melchester she would have found him difficult to ignore, she admitted wearily, but at least without it she would not have been forced to bear his gritty determination to exact what he considered to be his rightful dues. In fact she doubted that he would have spared her more than a passing glance. Men like Slade Ashford were used to having women fall over themselves to get to him, she thought bitterly; she doubted that he had ever in his whole life needed to do the chasing, and she was pretty sure that in normal circumstances the coldly indifferent attitude she wore like a protective armour against men of his type would have kept him at a distance—she had very little illusions and had always suspected that to men of his type the fruit which remained elusively out of reach at the top of the tree did not merit the effort involved in obtaining it when exactly the same fruit could be picked up off the ground quite freely.

She had no one but herself to blame for the fact that he was pursuing her; albeit for the most uncomplimentary of reasons, but the only thing she could do now was to make it abundantly clear to him that he aroused in her nothing but distaste and dislike.

Not given to self-delusion, she paused with one foot on the uppermost stair, a wry grimace pulling at the corners of her mouth as she asked herself inwardly how exactly she hoped to achieve that after last night's performance!

And it was no use trying to pretend that she had not responded to him, or that he had not recognised her response; he had made it only too plain that he had.

What was the matter with her, she asked herself despairingly; was she destined always to fall into the same trap? Was she mentally programmed to respond only to the type of man common sense warned her to avoid, or was it simply that at heart she was still every bit as foolishly vulnerable as her own niece?

Pushing aside the thought, she opened her bedroom door, and then stood frozen to the spot as she saw the man leaning indolently against the casement window.

'What are you doing in my room?' she demanded in freezing accents, her coat following her bag on to a chair as she walked determinedly towards him. Two yards away she came to an abrupt halt as she suddenly saw the yellow gleam of warning in his eyes.

'Slade . . .'

'Cut the outraged virtue,' he told her softly. 'It won't work.'

'Slade, I don't know what you're doing in here . . .' Anger had given way to fear, but she was determined not to give in to it. The suffocating silence seemed to smother her ability to think. All she was conscious of was Slade's reined in anger, glittering wolfishly in the unblinking eyes which tracked her every betraying movement.

'You know full well why I'm here,' he said at last. 'I don't like being led on and dropped flat; I don't like what you did to me in Melchester one little bit, and if you think I'm going to stand by and watch you do exactly the same thing to Tom Little, you can damned well think again! And before you say a word, I saw the two of you in the village.'

'You . . . but . . .'

'You didn't see me?' He laughed harshly. 'I'm hardly surprised—you had other things on your mind. I wouldn't have thought a country boy like Tom up to your weight, or is it amusing you to play the innocent butter-wouldn't-melt-in-my-mouth bit for him? Perhaps I ought to broaden his education a little, tell him what you're really like.'

'You couldn't!' Even to her own ears her voice sounded high and unnatural, but Chelsea refused to back down. 'You don't know what I'm really like,' she told him.

'Like hell!' Slade responded brutally, thrusting his shoulders away from the window and advancing on her. 'I know how you feel in a man's arms, how you melt against him . . . How you cheat . . . Well, you're not cheating on me, Chelsea!'

'I'm not trying to,' Chelsea told him bitterly. 'Look, I realise this might come as an outsize blow to your hugely inflated male ego, but it just so happens that you simply don't turn me on, and that's . . .'

'Liar.' He said it softly, his eyes glittering over her pale face, the word snarled past lips which suddenly looked hard and bitter. 'And I'll prove it to you if you like.'

She tried to move, but it was like being caught up in a dream, her whole body heavily weighted making escape impossible.

Overriding everything else was acute disbelief that merely seeing Tom kissing her had aroused this terrible anger in Slade. Some advice she had once read in a book about trying to keep calm in the face of aggression came back to her and she forced herself to keep resolutely still, flinching only when Slade's fingers bit painfully into her frail shoulderbones.

'Well?'

'It's perfectly possible for any experienced male to arouse a purely sexual response in a woman,' Chelsea told him icily.

'So you admit that I can arouse you?'

She hadn't admitted anything of the kind, but his fingers were moving disturbingly against her skin, anger giving way to a desire heightened by the emotionally charged atmosphere of the small room. A strangely lethargic sensation spread downwards from his caressing fingers; totally alien desire that knotted her stomach muscles into aching hunger. Panicking at the speed with which all her dearly held principles seemed to slide effortlessly away from her every time she came into close physical contact with Slade, Chelsea reached for the only weapon at hand.

'I admit it was amusing to let you think you could,' she drawled, trembling inwardly. 'Men seem to think that all they have to do is merely smile and mouth a few meaningless compliments and a girl is only too happy to go to bed with them.'

'When in reality what they really desire is more tangible evidence of admiration than mere compliments, is that it?' Slade's voice grated, somewhere above her ear. Fear flared inside her, but it was too late to back down now. 'So that's it!' She could sense the rage boiling up inside him. 'Lure your victim on and then drop him cold, first making sure that he'll get ample opportunity to see what he's missed out on, is that how it works? Is that why you ran out on me? Because you knew you were coming up here and that we'd be bound to meet again? Okay.' He shrugged before Chelsea could summon her appalled wits and deny his allegations. 'That's fine by me; I'm not averse to paying for my pleasure, it helps to tidy up a lot of messy ends and makes sure that you aren't left with any unwanted emotional involvements. So, what will it cost me to enjoy your delectable sexy body, Chelsea? A diamond necklace? A fur? An expensive holiday? I wouldn't be so crude as to suggest money. You see, I do appreciate the finer points of such negotiations . . .'

'From past experience!' Chelsea flung at him. Two spots of colour burned in her otherwise deathly pale face, disbelief and distaste warred inside her.

'As it happens you're wrong.' Slade had turned his back to her and Chelsea had no means of telling from the broad shoulders what he was thinking. 'Strange as you might find it,' he added coolly, 'you'll be the first woman I've ever had to bribe to share my bed. Normally . . .'

'They pay you?' Chelsea suggested sweetly, gasping with shock as he turned with the swiftness of a supine panther.

'I'm a man,' he told her contemptuously, 'with all that the word implies. I don't sell myself.'

'Neither do I,' Chelsea told him proudly.

'It's too late for backtracking now. You cheated on me, Chelsea, and that's something I don't allow anyone to get away with. First you're going to pay me what you owe me; then, if I think I'm getting value for money,' he told her insultingly, 'I'll consider coming to an arrangement with you, but first things first. Oh no,' he told her in a perfectly normal conversational voice as she turned for the door. 'I shouldn't try that—not unless you want me to get a good deal more impatient than I am already. Smile,' he commanded in a parody of a coaxing tone, 'like you did in Melchester.'

With sickening certainty Chelsea knew that she wasn't going to be allowed to leave the bedroom until she had satisfied his insane desire for revenge. He reached for her, and she started to tremble.

When he took her in his arms and feathered light kisses along her throat instead of the violent approach which she had expected, she didn't understand, and her bewilderment increased and showed in her eyes. Slade's mouth continued to move over her skin, subtly undermining her barriers. His hands moved from her shoulders over her back and then beneath the fine wool of her jumper, warm against her spine. She opened her mouth to protest when he unclipped her bra, but the words were muffled beneath the explosive warmth of his kiss. Weakly she closed her eyes. Sensation after alien sensation coursed over her.

'No!'

Her protest was totally ignored as Slade picked her up and carried her over to the bed, deftly removing her jumper before releasing her angrily trembling body.

He seemed totally impervious to her bitterness. Her skirt followed her other clothes on to the floor along with Slade's jacket.

'I want you,' he told her slowly, his eyes moving hotly over her body, 'and you're going to want me too, Chelsea, no matter how indifferent you've been to all those who came before me.'

It was then that she knew that he wasn't going to be satisfied with simply possessing her physically; he also wanted from her a response, total capitulation to his possession, and as she looked up at him studying the silky-skinned curves of her body Chelsea knew why she had run out of his flat and why she was trembling with sick fear now. It had nothing to do with Darren, and everything to do with the way her body reacted to Slade; the physical response merely looking at him aroused inside her; the terrible need to yield to the melting sensations spreading through her, to give herself up to him so completely that she became part of him.

Romantic novelists had a name for those feelings, she thought feverishly. They called them 'love', but it was impossible for her to love Slade Ashford. Love was something that grew with time and had nothing to do with this aching, raw desire that burned to fever pitch inside her.

'No!' she protested, blindly trying to escape from her own thoughts, fear closing her throat. 'No!'

'It's too late for that now,' Slade told her harshly. 'Although I don't doubt you mean it. Women like you always want to be in control, don't they? They like to be the aggressor, the hunter, the one who arouses desire but never truly experiences it.'

Chelsea could feel him watching her, his eyes moving slowly over the pale flesh he had exposed. Her heart hammered under her ribs, the effort of controlling her breathing making her throat ache with pain. She felt him shift his weight above her as he leaned on his side to study her, and then his hands were moving slowly over her body, stroking and caressing, banishing all her preconceived ideas and prejudices. She had simply never known that she was capable of feeling such pleasure. Hazily she tried to think back. Had she ever felt like this with Darren? She knew she hadn't. Her love for him had been an adolescent's, blind and adoring, completely free of the physical hunger leaping to life inside her now. Pride and pride alone was all that kept her own hands rigidly at her sides away from Slade. She must not touch him. The words hammered over and over again through her brain in a mindless litany which she used to try and blot out the sensations he was arousing, as though somehow she could divorce herself from the desire he was deliberately awakening.

She had expected, when he talked of her paying her dues, that he intended simply to possess her as a means of soothing his bruised ego, but she had underestimated him, she admitted; he wasn't going to be satisfied with simple physical domination.

'Open your eyes.'

The softly spoken command couldn't be ignored. She blinked at him hazily, gasping as his hands moved from her waist, upwards to cup her breasts, his fingers teasing her nipples. Panic stormed through her as she tried desperately to avoid his touch, squeezing her eyes closed as though by doing so she could obliterate the memory of how it had felt to have him touch her so intimately. Even when his hands returned to her waist she couldn't stop quivering. His mouth was against her throat, sending small shudders of pleasure along her skin. Despair and fear of her inability not to betray her feelings to him lent her the courage to say coolly, with just a hint of boredom in her voice,

'Look, why don't you just simply get it over with? I don't . . .'

'Have a lot of time?' he mocked, strangely unangered by her taunt. 'I like to take my pleasure slowly and enjoy it,' he said softly. 'Don't you?'

A suffocating heat seemed to rise up inside her, but whether it was engendered by what he had said or the way he was looking at her Chelsea didn't know.

His hands moved from her waist to her hips, caressing the fragile bones. Tension locked every muscle in her stomach. Lazily Slade slid one hand up to her breast, touching her as though he derived intense sensual satisfaction from the feel of her skin. His fingers looked brown against the paleness of her own flesh. His thumb stroked softly over her nipple and her nerve endings tightened like fine-drawn wire.

'Don't!' The word jerked involuntarily past her lips.

'Touch me, then,' Slade murmured provocatively, guiding her hand inside his shirt. His skin felt curiously vulnerable; soft and warm, the shadowing of hair on his chest grazing the tender flesh of her palm. She slid her hand experimentally along his ribs, startled to feel the powerful beat of his heart beneath her fingers. It was ridiculous to realise at her age that she had never touched a man so intimately. Her heartbeat sounded unnaturally loud in her ears, and somehow of its own accord her other hand started to explore the male breadth of his shoulders. Slade muttered something under his breath and discarded the shirt completely. His skin gleamed like burnished wood, tanned and healthy, and Chelsea's eyes seemed to cling hungrily to him, drinking in every feature. His hands framed her face, trapping her hands between them as her lips parted instinctively beneath his mouth.

Sensation after sensation rolled over her, all coherency lost as she was enveloped in a new world which contained only tactile sensuality.

Slade's hands held her hips, moulding them

against the aroused maleness of his thighs, his lips
exploring the soft slope of her shoulder and then
moving downwards along the curve of her breast,
his face buried against the warmth of her.

Something seemed to constrict her breathing, an
unbearable tension holding her in its grip. Dimly
she was aware of a car door slamming, but its
meaning didn't penetrate, until Slade swore
suddenly and thrust himself away from her, his
face unreadable in the darkness as he commented
sardonically, 'Your guardian angel has suddenly
come back on duty, and with a vengeance! Mrs
Rudge is back,' he added when she continued to
look befuddled. He laughed softly. 'Perhaps it's no
bad thing after all; it might do you good to suffer
a little of what you put me through when you ran
out on me that night. Dreams are no substitute for
reality, as I'm sure you'll soon realise.'

His eyes rested on the provocative thrust of her
breasts and Chelsea reached hurriedly for her
jumper, shame searing her as she acknowledged
how dangerously—and how easily—she had succumbed to his sensual expertise. Even now when
her mind was acknowledging the providence which
had brought Mrs Rudge back, her body was
treacherously aching for Slade's touch. She
glanced quickly at him, overwhelmed by a sudden
urge to reach out and touch him; to feel the thick
darkness of his hair beneath her fingers, and the
warmth of his body against hers, and the
knowledge of what those feelings meant rocked
her back on her heels.

CHAPTER SIX

CHRISTMAS drew nearer. Chelsea had refused the invitation from the farm, explaining that she wanted to complete her work on the tapestry as soon as possible.

The hours she spent up at Darkwater were becoming oases of calm which allowed her to recharge her batteries in readiness for the time she was obliged to spend with Slade.

To her surprise he had made no further attempts to be alone with her, or to remind her of his threats, and at first she thought he had abandoned his plans, until she realised that he was playing a careful waiting game. He desired her. It was obvious in the way he looked at her without saying a word, his eyes on her body, but instead of feeling flattered Chelsea felt only fear. If he had merely been seeking revenge she felt she could have coped, but his desire was something against which she had no armour, and she sensed that his need to make her capitulate to him was the greater because of it.

And then there were her own feelings. It was no longer possible for her to dismiss the way she felt whenever he touched her, and she knew that if it hadn't been for Darren, she would have succumbed to Slade's charismatic sensuality long before now.

The local people seemed to like him. Tom told her that they were saying in the village that it made a change to have a 'Black Percy' in residence who had their interests at heart.

She and Mrs Rudge must be the only two people who still held out against him, Chelsea reflected bitterly, and she told herself that she was glad she had the common sense not to be taken in by what she knew to be mere surface charm.

Later in the afternoon she had an unexpected opportunity to see the full potency of that charm and its effect on the female sex. The tapestry was responding even better than she had hoped to her ministrations. The dyed wools and silks were a perfect match to the existing threads, and Chelsea had spent a very enjoyable morning re-stitching the helmet and visor of a Crusader before turning her attention to a scene depicting the women's long wait for their men to return.

A woman with golden hair almost as long as the fabled Rapunzel's stood in the embrasure of a tower, children at her skirts. The wife of the Crusader? Chelsea wondered—but surely she would have had her hair covered. As she stitched industriously at the golden plaits she found herself weaving daydreams around the stiffly sewn figures. She was a young girl of the household who had been in love with the knight from girlhood. He had married for reasons of financial and political gain—a marriage arranged by his family. There were children of the marriage and the girl had been appointed their nurse. The knight had ridden off to the Crusade and now he was coming back, and the young girl had the unhappy task of telling him that his wife had died of childbed fever in his absence.

He would need to marry again, Chelsea reflected, a mother for his children and a chatelaine for the castle, and who better than the girl who had adored him for so long?

She sighed. Life wasn't like that. The girl would probably end her days unwed while the man would marry again for financial advantage. If she was lucky the girl might find herself sharing his bed one night when his wife's back was turned; a crust thrown to a starving dog.

Chelsea lifted her head as she heard the sound of a car outside. Doors slammed and then there were voices in the hallway below her. She froze as she heard Slade saying lazily, 'Most of the structural work is finished now—but I don't need to tell you that.'

She wasn't quite sure what she ought to do. Slade and whoever was with him were probably unaware that she was in the gallery working and that she could hear every word of their conversation whether she wanted to or not. If she made her presence known it might seem as though she were trying to foist herself off on them, and if she didn't . . .

She was still debating what to do when she heard Slade add, 'But of course it's the tapestry you've really come to see. I believe Miss Evans is working on it upstairs.'

'A marvellous find,' a husky feminine voice agreed. 'We couldn't believe our luck. That combined with the money you've endowed on Darkwater should ensure its unkeep for the future.'

'I hope so,' Chelsea heard Slade say as they

walked towards the stairs. 'This house has been the home of my family for a long time. I hadn't realised how neglected it had become, which was my own fault, I suppose. I visited my uncle pretty regularly, but the place was always locked up, and somehow there was never the time.'

'It's quite a common story,' another male voice agreed. 'A few more years and we might not have been so lucky.'

'What I can't understand is why your uncle allowed the house to deteriorate so much,' the husky female voice chimed in. 'By all accounts he was a relatively wealthy man.'

'Yes, he was,' Slade agreed. 'I think the root of the problem lay in the fact that he had no direct heir to leave the place to. The fact that he never married was his own choice, and I don't honestly believe he regretted it, or the knowledge that the place would one day come to me, until very recently. Some of the blame must lie with me. I was in New York for six months when I wasn't able to see him. When I returned I was appalled to see how much he had aged; his memory was seriously impaired, and with it, I suspect, his judgment. He seemed to be obsessed by the fact that I wasn't able to perpetuate the Percy name. He even wanted me to adopt it, but as I pointed out to him, I owed it to my father to stay an Ashford. My father was never made particularly welcome up here and some people never forgave him for the fact that he was a southerner.'

Mrs Rudge, thought Chelsea immediately. Had she deliberately tried to poison Slade's uncle against him? She could easily imagine her doing so. The housekeeper was almost fanatical in her belief that the 'old master', as she called him, should have had sons of his own.

As she heard feet on the stairs she quickly folded the piece of the tapestry she had been working on and stood up.

'Ah, there you are.'

Slade's smile was coolly businesslike. At his side was an elegant blonde, her hair drawn sleekly back off her face, her expensive tweed skirt and cashmere sweater proclaiming her 'county' origins. She extended her hand to Chelsea with a thin smile, barely touching her fingers.

'Ah yes,' she murmured, consulting some papers she had with her. 'You are employed by Jerome Francis, I believe?'

'Yes, I am,' Chelsea agreed. 'At the moment I'm working on the tapestry.'

'And doing an excellent job on it,' the third member of the trio praised warmly. While Slade and his female companion had approached her he had turned his attention to the tapestry, which for ease of working Chelsea had spread out on a long refectory table.

'How badly damaged was it?' Warm brown eyes surveyed Chelsea approvingly. Older than Slade, she placed the man somewhere in his late thirties, and she warmed to his admiration and appreciation of the rare tapestry, as he studied it closely, listening to her explaining the preparatory work which had been necessary before she could start repairs.

'Geoff and Fiona are from the National Trust,' Slade explained to her. 'They were in the area and wanted to come and see how work was progressing.'

'And to enjoy that lunch you promised us when you came to York,' Fiona reminded him provocatively, ignoring both Chelsea and the tapestry, until Geoff directed her attention to the latter and she was obliged to study it.

It was plain to Chelsea that the blonde girl knew little or nothing about the work, and she was forced to quell a swift stab of resentment when the pink-tipped nails rested lightly against Slade's jacket-clad arm as she asked him to explain the scenes depicted, knowing that the girl had next to no interest in the work and that all she wanted to do was to focus Slade's attention solely upon herself.

They made a stunning pair, Chelsea was forced to acknowledge grudgingly. Fiona was tall and slender, almost fragile when compared to the lean muscularity of Slade's maleness. Watching their two heads bent over the tapestry, dark against fair, she was appalled by the sudden surge of emotion that swept her. Try as she might she couldn't drag her eyes from Slade's lean fingers and immaculately kept nails as he pointed out various features of the tapestry to his companion.

The way Fiona fawned over him was sickening, Chelsea told herself, trying to convince herself that it was sheer female revulsion at such a lack of pride by a member of her sex that was responsible for the emotions raging inside her—and as for Slade himself, his smug acceptance of her admiration as his due just underlined how right she had been in her initial reading of his character.

They deserved one another, she told herself crossly, and she wished them joy of their lunch. She only wished it was dinner they were having together and then she would not be forced to endure Slade's silent scrutiny at the dinner table herself. Her stomach lurched suddenly as she thought of Slade and Fiona dining together; leaving together perhaps to return to the seclusion of Fiona's room.

'You obviously enjoy your work.' The quiet comment cut across her thoughts, jerking her into awareness that the gently smiling man at her side had been observing the way she was watching Slade and Fiona.

'I do,' she told him honestly. 'Very much.'

'You certainly know a good deal about your own family history,' she heard Fiona saying admiringly to Slade. 'Who is this?' she asked, pointing to the golden-haired figure Chelsea had been working on when they interrupted her.

For some reason Chelsea found herself holding her breath, unwilling to have the fairy tale she had spun around the fair-haired girl broken by the cold hard facts of truth, and yet experiencing an unwilling interest to know who she had been.

'That,' Slade told them, 'is the woman one of my ancestors brought back with him from the Crusades. The story goes that at the time he was betrothed to the Lady Alys Percy but that he fell hopelessly in love with Damask in the Holy Land and brought her back with him intending to marry her.

'She had told him that her parents had been killed by the infidels, and that she had been struggling to care for her infant brother and sister on her own. Out of love for her Roland swore a vow of chastity towards her until he could make her his wife.

'When he told his elder brother that he wanted to marry her, he laughed in his face. Damask was a whore, he told him, and her supposed "brother and sister" in reality her own bastards. He himself had first-hand knowledge that she was nothing more than a common harlot, he told Roland.'

'What happened to her?' Chelsea demanded huskily. It seemed to her that the girl's blue eyes reproached them from the canvas, and there was an aching pain in the region of her own heart.

'She threw herself from the battlements of the castle when Roland faced her with the truth,' Slade told her unemotionally. 'As a penance for his sins Roland raised her bastards along with his own children, although they always maintained that she was their sister and not their mother. She'd trained them from babyhood to lie, I suppose.'

'Why?' Chelsea heard herself saying fiercely. 'Why couldn't she have been telling the truth?'

'Because Roland's brother had indisputable proof that she wasn't,' Slade told her, watching her with narrowed eyes which seemed to ask why she should be taking such an interest in a girl who had lived and died over eight hundred years before.

'He might have been lying,' Chelsea retorted stubbornly. 'It was only his word against hers.'

'Possible, but hardly likely,' Slade argued smoothly. 'What would he have to gain?'

'Perhaps Miss Evans is trying to suggest that he
wanted the girl for himself,' Fiona interrupted,
giving Chelsea an acid little smile, plainly annoyed
that Slade's attention had been diverted away from
herself, her expression saying that she had grown
bored with the subject of the girl. 'I want to see the
rest of the house,' she commanded, drawing her
arm through Slade's and turning her back on
Chelsea.

Geoff went with them, and Chelsea told herself
she was glad to be alone.

I believe you, she found herself wanting to
comfort the girl of her imagination, but instead
she forced herself to concentrate on her work,
instead of daydreaming about events so deeply
buried in the past that they would never know the
truth.

Of the trio only Geoff returned to say goodbye
to her. He was smiling when he told her that he
had to return to York instead of joining the others
for lunch. 'I'm sure Fiona won't miss my
company,' he told Chelsea, 'although I might have
been tempted to stay if you were joining us.'

Slade appeared just as Geoff was leaving, his
expression sardonic as he bent his head to mutter
so that only she could hear, 'You just can't resist
trying, can you? First me, then Tom, and now
Geoff.'

'My mother always told me there was safety in
numbers,' Chelsea riposted sweetly, adding for
good measure, with a limpid smile, 'I do hope you
enjoy your lunch.'

His drawled, 'I'm sure I shall,' made her stab the
point of her needle clumsily into her finger,

drawing a tiny dot of blood. When they had gone she felt strangely restless, unable to blot from her mind the memory of the possessive way Fiona had clung to Slade's arm. What was the matter with her? she asked herself crossly. Surely she wasn't jealous? She stopped as though she had been turned to stone, shivering with realisation of the truth. She was jealous—bitterly and helplessly so. And why? Because she couldn't bear to see Slade touch or hold anyone but herself. The enormity of the truth was a death blow to her pride. She had fallen in love with Slade Ashford.

She tried to tell herself that it simply wasn't true, but once admitted the truth could not be banished. Right from the start it had been there, she knew now, although she had cloaked her feelings in anger and indignation, forcing herself to feel contempt and trying to convince herself that her love was merely sexual attraction, while all the time her feelings had grown stronger and stronger. If she didn't love him she would never have reacted in his arms the way she had done. Not even Darren had made her feel like that. She bit hard on her bottom lip. Now more than ever it was imperative that she finish her work and leave as quickly as she could. Thank goodness Slade was leaving before Christmas for New York. Chelsea trembled convulsively, suddenly aware of how desperately important it was that she should prevent him from carrying out his threats against her.

She had already sensed that he was playing a waiting game with her. She had already hopelessly betrayed the fact that she wasn't indifferent to him, and he, thinking her as sexually experienced as he was himself, was no doubt waiting until her desire became too much for her and she abandoned herself completely to him. He wasn't going to be satisfied with simply possessing her body, but even if he had been she knew she could not afford to let that happen.

Slade was no fool. Once he discovered that before him there had been no other men he was bound to put two and two together. She could explain away her initial behaviour with the truth if she had to, but how was she to explain why after years of not responding to sexual overtures she should suddenly succumb to his? She suspected it would be impossible to convince him that it was merely desire; her responses to him were too betraying. He was a man used to coaxing foolish girls into believing they were in love with him, he would have no difficulty in guessing what had happened to her, and she simply could not bear that, she decided grimly, remembering the torture of the humiliation she had endured over Darren. There was no way she was going to go through all that again, and with Darren it had simply been infatuation. With Slade it went far deeper, and she was forced to acknowledge that even though her mind told her that she ought to feel nothing but contempt for him, her heart refused to listen.

It brought Chelsea no pleasure to eat alone at the Dower House, suspecting as she did that Slade was still with Fiona.

She tried to settle down after her meal to watch television, but found it almost impossible to concentrate on the small screen. Mrs Rudge always returned to her own rooms in the evening, and knowing that her company would not be welcome Chelsea wandered into the library thinking that a book might help to keep her mind off her problems.

A history of the Borders caught her eye and she picked it up. Rather than be discovered by Slade when he returned, waiting up for his return and giving him the satisfaction of seeing just how much his absence had affected her, Chelsea took the book up to bed with her.

A warm bath helped to relax her over-strained nerves, and acting on impulse she pulled on her dressing gown and went downstairs to the study to telephone Ann.

The very sound of her sister's voice had a soothing effect upon her. No, Kirsty was showing no ill effects from their interference over Slade Ashford, Ann assured her. In fact she seemed happier than she had been for a long time. 'Possibly because we're beginning to give in over this drama school business. She's nowhere near as sensitive or vulnerable as you, Chelsea,' Ann admitted. 'We saw her in the school play last week, and I have to admit she was absolutely marvellous. Her English teacher had a word with us, and apparently he thinks she has real talent. Ralph says we owe it to her to give her a chance, but we're both adamant that she has to take a secretarial course first just so that she has something to fall back on.'

Although she was relieved to discover that Kirsty seemed to be getting over her infatuation for Slade, Chelsea acknowledged as she returned to her bedroom that it altered nothing as far as she was concerned. Even if he had not been the sort of man she despised, what hope did she have that he could possibly love her? None at all, she admitted wryly, climbing into bed and picking up her book, and if she had any common sense she would put him right out of her mind. But when had common sense ever had anything to do with love?

It was the low purr of the Ferrari engine that woke her, her senses instantly alert as she stared through the darkness to the luminous dial of her alarm clock. Two in the morning. Pain knifed through her. It didn't take much imagination to guess how Slade had spent his evening. Perhaps he would now ignore her. It would be better if he did, she acknowledged, because if he continued his relentless assault on her defences she could place no dependence on resisting him. She shuddered, contemplating his sardonic mockery if he ever discovered the truth, praying that he never would. How he would laugh when he discovered her vulnerability! She heard him coming upstairs and froze as for a second he seemed to pause outside her door. Her heart thudded painfully against her ribs as she held her breath, but then the footsteps moved on, and she told herself that she must have imagined that faint hesitation outside her room.

There was no sign of Slade at breakfast, and Mrs Rudge offered no explanation for his absence.

Chelsea decided to drive down to the village to replenish her diminishing stocks of shampoo and soap. As she parked the car and climbed out she saw Sandy coming out of the chemists and hailed

the other girl cheerfully. Sandy flushed, and
Chelsea gained the impression that she was none
too pleased to see her.

When Sandy asked curtly, 'Isn't Tom with you?'
Chelsea was puzzled.

'No,' she told her. 'Why should he be?'

Sandy shrugged and looked away. 'Well, you
two are something of an item round here. It's no
great secret either that Mrs Little has been wanting
Tom to get married for ages. She's longing for
grandchildren and a domesticated daughter-in-
law.'

'I think you're rather jumping to conclusions,'
Chelsea told her mildly. 'Tom and I are
friends . . .'

'You mean you're not interested in him now
you've got bigger fish to fry in the shape of Slade
Ashford,' Sandy burst out bitterly, pushing past
her and hurrying down the street, leaving Chelsea
to stare unhappily after her.

Sandy's reference to Slade had given the truth
away. The poor girl was jealous, and if she did but
know it, with scant cause. Poor Sandy, Chelsea
reflected as she made her purchases. She had liked
her and had hoped they could have become
friends. She sometimes felt lonely at Darkwater
and would have welcomed the company of another
girl. She missed her chats with Ann and the
cheerful company of Kirsty. She was tempted to
hurry after Sandy and tell her the truth, but she
doubted that the younger girl would have believed
her. She hero-worshipped Slade and would
undoubtedly believe that Chelsea was simply
trying to discredit him.

The sight of Tom's Range Rover outside the house as she drove towards it helped to lift Chelsea's spirits considerably.

Mrs Rudge smiled grimly when she opened the door and imparted the information that Tom was waiting for her in the study.

He grinned when he saw her, and sensing that he was going to kiss her, Chelsea moved away, wondering how on earth she could explain to him that all they could be was friends, without betraying her own love for Slade.

'You're a welcome sight for a poor farmer,' he teased, studying her slim form in cord jeans in a rich dark blue toned with a blue and rust checked Vyella blouse and a blouson cord jacket which matched her jeans.

The wind had whipped her hair into soft tendrils round her face and the pure Border air had brought new colour to her cheeks. Blusher was something she had quickly discovered she didn't need up here. Although she was unaware of it the rich blue of her cords and jacket emphasised the colour of her eyes, and Tom observed her with male appreciation as she waited for him to speak.

'I know you claim you can't leave your work long enough to spend Christmas Day with us,' he began, 'but this time I won't take no for an answer. I've got tickets for the Young Farmers' Ball—quite a social highlight in these parts. It's held on Boxing Day night. Formal gear's the order of the day, and it's normally very good . . .'

Chelsea frowned. 'Oh Tom, I can't,' she apologised. 'I haven't got anything formal to wear with me.'

Neither of them had been aware of the front door opening and closing as they spoke, nor of the grim expression in Slade Ashford's eyes as he overheard their conversation.

Tom was still struggling for the right words to overcome Chelsea's objections, mentally cursing himself for ever mentioning formal evening attire, when Slade walked slowly into the room.

'Nothing to wear?' he mocked, making it plain that he had overheard. 'Surely that can't be true? Or had you forgotten this?' he added cruelly. 'You left it in my room.'

Chelsea's expression betrayed her immediately she saw the crumpled blue silk dress he was holding in his hands, and too late she saw the bitterness in Tom's eyes, and knew that he had seen the instant recognition in hers.

'Tom . . .' she started to protest as he turned away, 'I can explain.'

'Go ahead,' Slade told her savagely, 'tell him exactly how this came to be in my possession. Or have you forgotten? In that case let me refresh your memory a little.'

'Is it yours?' Tom asked dully, and even though she longed to plead with him to listen to her, Chelsea could only nod her head, knowing the conclusions he must be drawing from her admission and hating Slade for subjecting her to such humiliation.

'I see.' The two words fell between them like flat hard pebbles. 'I have been a fool, haven't I?' Tom said bitterly. 'And I thought you were different—innocent and untouched.' He laughed harshly, 'I couldn't have been more wrong! It won't last, you know,' he told Chelsea. 'Ask Mrs Rudge—she knows all about Percy men. Thirty years she worked for Matt Percy, every one of them hoping he'd marry her, but he never did. She was good enough for him to take to his bed before she married Bert Rudge, but marriage—no way!'

Chelsea couldn't bring herself to look at Slade. Tom's allegations were too convincing to be denied as mere gossip, and Chelsea suspected that Slade must have known the situation and why Mrs Rudge was so bitterly opposed to him. No doubt all those years she had been thinking not simply that Matt Percy's own son ought to succeed him but that that child could have been hers.

'You don't have to make any excuses any more,' Tom said quietly as he walked towards the door. 'I quite understand the position.'

Chelsea said nothing until she heard the Range Rover engine fire. All the colour had left her face, and her fingernails bit into her palms as she fought for self-control.

She felt Slade move behind her and out of the corner of her eye saw him pick up her dress.

'I hope you're satisfied!' she managed finally in a thick choked voice. 'How could you do that?'

'Quite easily,' came the urbane response, 'but I'm not satisfied, as you put it, Chelsea, and I won't be until I have you in my bed, responding to me without a thought in your greedy little head apart from how much you want my hands on your body.'

'I'll never want you like that,' Chelsea told him half hysterically, 'Do you hear me? Never!'

She turned towards the door, hating him as she had never hated anyone in her whole life—not even Darren—unable to forget the look in Tom's eyes. She had thought Tom was his friend, and yet he had destroyed his pride as callously as he might crush an insect underfoot.

'How could you do that to Tom?' she demanded from the door, her eyes blazingly blue in her pale face. In her book only one emotion could justify such a vindictive action, and that was the same searingly painful jealousy she experienced whenever she thought of him with another woman. She was appalled to discover that he could so easily destroy another human being, totally without compunction, merely as a means of inflicting pain on her, and for what? Simply so that he could reinforce his threats and save the tiny bruise she had inflicted on his ego.

'You're despicable!' she told him bitterly. 'To have hurt Tom like that. In a wildly jealous lover your behaviour might have been excusable, but . . .'

There was an odd expression in his eyes, a tenseness about his jaw that warned Chelsea she was treading on dangerous ground.

'But what?' he prompted softly, watching her.

'But you have no excuse,' Chelsea told him tiredly, the adrenalin anger and fear had released into her blood suddenly ceasing, leaving her feeling drained and exhausted. 'And Tom . . .'

'Forget Tom,' he told her brutally. 'He'll find solace soon enough, and with someone far better equipped to make him happy than you.'

'Who?' Chelsea demanded, too stunned by his comment to stop the word from forming.

'Sandy,' Slade told her unequivocally.

Chelsea stared at him, unable to believe her ears. Was he seriously suggesting that Tom should marry Sandy when it was perfectly obvious that the poor girl was in love with Slade? No doubt he didn't want to be accused of callously disregarding the feelings of a local girl, Chelsea thought bitterly. Her parents were obviously his friends and he was cynical enough to believe in the maxim that it was always wiser to play away from home.

There was simply nothing she could say to him to convey the depth of her contempt.

As she swept out of the study only she knew that her senses had betrayed her by relaying a detailed awareness of the lean bulk of Slade's body clothed in close-fitting black jeans and a matching shirt open at the throat. For a moment her eyes rested incautiously on the buckle fastening the belt encircling tautly male hips, and then she was through the door, her heart pounding against her chest, a tight unbearable pain squeezing tears into her eyes and locking her throat.

CHAPTER SEVEN

'You realise you'll be alone here over Christmas?'

'Yes.' Chelsea made the monosyllabic reply and then concentrated on her breakfast coffee. For two days she had studiously avoided Slade as best she could. Two days when she had constantly been tempted to pick up the phone and ring Tom to explain the truth and had always at the last moment quailed. Perhaps in some ways it was better that he thought the worst of her, she admitted tiredly. There could after all have been no future for them, but Slade's extraordinary behaviour still left a bitter aftertaste in her mouth and she could hardly bear to bring herself to speak to him.

'Mrs Rudge will be away,' Slade reminded her, 'and this house is remote. More snow is forecast.'

Chelsea glanced out of the window at the white landscape. It had started snowing the previous day and she hadn't been able to suppress a tiny thrill at the magical quality of the fluffy whiteness drifting down to cover the earth. A white Christmas; the embodiment of all her childhood dreams, but this year she would be spending it alone.

Mrs Rudge was leaving after breakfast to spend Christmas with her sister, and Slade was going in the afternoon. It would be a relief to be alone in many ways, Chelsea admitted; at least then she could abandon the constant struggle to conceal how she felt from Slade. His behaviour by rights ought to have killed what she felt for him, but it hadn't, a fact which only increased her fear.

She risked an upwards glance and wished she hadn't when she saw the open mockery in the dark green eyes. Thank goodness he would soon be gone, and there would be no more mornings like this to undermine her shaky self-control.

He was dressed casually, a checked shirt open at the throat revealing enough of his chest to remind her of how the dark hairs shadowing it had scraped erotically against her own skin. Faded jeans hugged his hips, reminding her that he was no callow boy but an intensely sensual and experienced man. Her blood seemed to pound against her veins, her stomach muscles contracting in vain desire. Her eyes clung to his tanned forearms. He glanced absently at his watch and she looked hurriedly away. He had showered before coming down for breakfast and the clean male scent of his skin seemed to reach out and envelop her. His hair was still damp, and curled slightly against his nape, and she longed to reach up and touch it; to have the freedom to slide her hands inside his shirt and feel the warmth of his body, pulsating as urgently as her own.

She pushed her coffee away unfinished and stumbled to her feet, her face pale, stunned by the awareness of how quickly everything but Slade had lost any meaning for her. At least with Darren she had retained some sanity, some sense of what was right and wrong, some pride. Her skin seemed to burn with strange tension as though she were about to come down with a fever and in an illuminating and bitter moment of self-knowledge she knew that if he were to touch her now there was simply no way she would be able to stop herself from responding, from begging him to make love to her.

She was dimly aware of him getting to his feet and saying something to her, but it seemed to reach her from a distance, muffled and indecipherable above the roaring sound that reminded her of that heard from a seashell held against the ear.

She took a step forward and stumbled blindly

halted by the swiftly cruel grasp of his hands on her waist. Her whole body shook violently with reaction, her teeth chattering even though she felt quite hot.

'Chelsea!' This time his voice reached her, its crisply angered tone penetrating her fog of fear. 'What's the matter? Are you ill?'

She couldn't speak. Her throat seemed to have closed up and she felt perilously close to tears. She longed to beg him to set her free. Her skin felt scorched with heat where he touched it. Like him, she was wearing jeans, her boots already on preparatory to the walk to Darkwater which she felt was safer than risking the car in present weather conditions. Overnight the snow had frozen, and more was forecast, as evidenced by the leaden sky, with its ominously pink tinge. The hills seemed closer, sharply outlined in white against the dove grey sky, and she wondered absently if all Tom's sheep were safe.

Tom! Guilt nagged at her. She ought to ring him up and explain, but she knew she wouldn't.

'Chelsea! Damn you, don't faint on me!' she heard Slade mutter, raising his voice to call the housekeeper. 'Chelsea, what's wrong?' He was shaking her, and she hated herself for the way her body exulted in even his briefest touch.

The dining room door swung open and Mrs Rudge came in. Chelsea watched her expression change from hauteur to dismay as she took in the scene.

'Lord save us, she's not ill, is she?' she heard her asking Slade. 'Well I can't stay to look out to her. Made my arrangements I have.'

'I can look after myself,' Chelsea managed to croak, her speech mercifully restored to her. 'I just felt a little light-headed. It's nothing—just something I've always been prone to,' she lied.

'I'll go and make you a nice cup of tea, that will do the trick,' Mrs Rudge pronounced, darting a disapproving glare at Slade as she left.

'I'm fine now,' Chelsea told him, praying that he would release her. His hands still gripped her waist and he was close enough for her to be able to see the small flecks of yellow which gave his eyes their golden greenness.

'I don't like leaving you here alone,' he told her abruptly. 'This place is too remote. Are you sure you're all right? You're stubborn enough to pretend you are when you aren't.'

'Stubborn?' Chelsea laughed weakly, pushing back the weight of her hair as it swung forward. Her movements faltered as she saw the way Slade was watching her. There was no mistaking or disguising the naked hunger flaring to life in his eyes, and just for a second she contemplated throwing all caution to the winds and taking the tiny step which was all that would be needed to carry her into his arms.

Between one heartbeat and the next she realised the supreme folly of what she had so nearly done, and more to punish herself than Slade she lashed out bitterly.

'Quite a wasted opportunity as far as you're concerned, isn't it? If you weren't going to New York you'd have me completely at your mercy, wouldn't you, and ample opportunity to carry out your threats.'

Slade's gritted, 'Don't tempt me,' brought her back to shocked sanity, and her eyes dilated with fear as he added gratingly, 'You owe me this if nothing else.'

She wasn't given the chance to evade the brutal strength of the arms that bound her to him, curving her body against his, and forcing her neck back until she thought it would snap under the pressure. Her vulnerability only seemed to fuel his anger. There was no mercy in the mouth that closed hotly over her own, forcing her lips to yield and part, and she was forced into the ignominious position of having to cling helplessly to his shoulders, totally unable to defend herself from the humiliation he was inflicting.

As though he suddenly sensed that hurting her would not achieve the result he desired, Chelsea felt the pressure of his hands lessen, one slowly massaging the tense bones of her spine before grasping a handful of her hair and forcing her head up to meet the savage scrutiny of his eyes. Dull dark colour lay along the sharp angles of his cheekbones, a raw passion smouldering in the tense green depths of the eyes fastened on her.

For a moment time seemed to stand still before hurtling her dizzyingly along a path she knew instinctively could only lead to pain.

'Damn you, Chelsea,' Slade swore softly, 'but you will respond to me.'

He bent his head and she shivered in mindless pleasure as his lips moved delicately along the pure exposed line of her throat where he had pushed aside her hair. His tongue traced the shape of her ear while his thumb stroked the vulnerable hollow behind it. His lips were moving softly over her face, constricting her breathing. Panic flared up inside her as she recognised her overwhelming need to reach out and touch him, to melt and be devoured by the heated passion he was fuelling.

She sobbed helplessly, trying to smother the sound, and knew it was too late when she saw the wild elation gleaming in his eyes and felt the hungry urgency of his mouth as it skilfully drew from hers the response she had tried to deny him.

Caution and common sense faded into nothing. There was only the wild surging of her blood and her instinctive response to Slade's urgent possession of her mouth. Her arms were round his neck, her fingers buried in the thick softness of his hair. Slade's hands slid down to her hips, holding her against him and deliberately making her aware of his desire for her.

Drugged and bemused by the sensations he was arousing, Chelsea knew how completely her barriers were down; how she would ache for him when he was gone and desperately recall these moments.

When Slade heard Mrs Rudge returning he released her smoothly, triumph glittering in his eyes.

'Think about me when I'm gone,' he mocked her as the door opened.

Colour flared in Chelsea's pale face. She had given him the response he desired and he had every reason to feel triumphant. Released from his arms, she hated herself for giving way to her love for him, and was only thankful that she would be long gone from Blackwater when he eventually returned. She had told herself long ago, after the débâcle with Darren, that she would never give herself to anyone without a mutually shared love, and only she knew just how close she had come to abandoning that fiercely held principle.

To her dismay Slade insisted on driving her down to the house when she had drunk her tea. She was trembling with nervous dread when he brought the car to a halt outside, but to her inward chagrin, he simply opened her door for her and allowed her to alight without making any move to touch her, his knowing, 'Disappointed?' bringing a dark flush of colour to her skin as she turned her back on him and struggled through the snow which had drifted by the doors.

As she worked her thoughts returned to him, time and time again distracting her to the point where she had to stop working or risk making mistakes.

Somehow today the old house felt lonelier than it had ever done in the past, and although she told herself that her response was merely psychological because she knew that she was alone, Chelsea could not banish the melancholy feelings that engulfed her. As she worked on the tapestry her thoughts kept straying to Slade. At two in the afternoon she wondered if he had yet reached the airport at Newcastle and what time his flight took off. Her skin burned with heat when she remembered her total response to his kiss, and her hands shook so much that it was almost impossible for her to hold her needle.

By three it had gone so dark that she was forced to switch on the powerful light she used for working, and the oil-filled radiator she used to heat her working space no longer seemed to generate enough heat to keep her warm. When she went to fill the electric kettle she used to make hot drinks with she realised that it was snowing again, and she shivered in anticipation of the long walk back to the house.

By three-thirty she was so cold that she decided it was pointless working on any longer, and she wished she had brought the car, then she could have put the tapestry in it and taken it back to the Dower House to work on in greater comfort. With the house empty she could have used the dining room table to spread the tapestry out on, but it was too late to regret not bringing the car now.

Perhaps if the snow stopped she could return later, she promised herself, trying not to feel guilty at stopping work so early in the afternoon.

Although she had removed her boots and placed them by the radiator on her arrival they were still damp from the snow she had trudged through in the morning, and now too late she wished she had had the forethought to buy herself a pair of wellingtons.

An icy wind knifed through her when she stepped outside, completely nullifying the protection of her cream jacket. This snow had none of the pretty softness of yesterday's, she reflected as she hunched forward, head down against the driving white onslaught of the blizzard.

Normally it took half an hour to cover the distance between the two houses, and Chelsea was overwhelmingly grateful for the familiar rows of elms lining the drive as she trudged through the quickly deepening snow, otherwise she was sure she would have lost her way in the white wilderness the world had become. Tiny particles of snow stung her cheeks and nose, despite her boots and gloves her feet and hands were frozen, her leg muscles aching from the effort of trudging through the wind-drifted snow.

At last, to her relief, the Dower House appeared, like an illustration on a Christmas card.

She opened the door thankfully, and reached down to pull off her boots, but her hands were far too cold to enable her to do so. Brushing off as much of the snow as she could, she trudged wearily upstairs. She would just try and get warm and then she would take them off. Walking through the snow seemed to have drained away all her energy and she felt curiously tired.

The door to Slade's bedroom stood open and as she walked past it she was overwhelmed by a desire to go in. What was she? an inner voice demanded in self-mockery; an infatuation-crazed adolescent yearning for just the merest glimpse of where her idol laid his weary head?

Clothes lay discarded on the old-fashioned half-tester bed, and Chelsea dimly recognised the jeans and shirt Slade had been wearing that morning. Like someone in a trance she walked towards the bed and picked up the checked shirt, holding it against her cheek. The male scent of Slade's body still clung to the fabric and her senses responded immediately to it, desire shuddering through her as she tried not to give in to her need for him.

She was still clutching the shirt, her eyes shadowed with desire, when the door to the ensuite bathroom was abruptly thrust open and Slade emerged, his hair damp, a towel knotted carelessly over his hips.

He was the first to recover himself, stretching out a long arm to recover his shirt, his expression unreadable as he said softly, 'Turns you on, does it? Try imagining how I felt with nothing but that damned dress of yours and a raging sense of frustration.'

'You're still here.' Stupidly it was all she could think of to say.

'So I am,' Slade agreed evenly, 'and aren't you the lucky one—I'm staying here, and so tonight instead of going to bed with my shirt you can go to bed with me. I'm tired of playing games, Chelsea,' he told her brutally. 'I want you and if you had a single shred of honesty you'd admit that you want me too, but that isn't how you like things to be, is it? You don't normally want your victims, do you? When was the last time you went to bed with a man you genuinely wanted physically?' he asked her softly. 'Or can't you even remember?'

He was reaching for her, droplets of moisture clinging sleekly to his skin, and Chelsea knew with a terrible sense of finality that this time there would be no escape. The knowledge galvanised her into action. With a small tormented cry she pushed past him, almost running downstairs as she ignored his angry command to her to stop.

The front door yielded to her touch, flurries of snow blinding her as she darted instinctively towards the tall line of elms, everything but the need to escape the ultimate humiliation of having

Slade discover her love for him driven from her mind.

How long she had been running heedlessly before she realised that she had lost sight of the elms lining the drive, Chelsea didn't know, but when she spun round despairingly looking for these landmarks the landscape had turned into a blinding white wilderness filled only by the tiny ice-sharp slivers of snow tormenting her skin. She turned awkwardly and wrenched her foot so painfully that it hurt to put any weight upon it, and she started to shiver in the realisation of her folly. She had no idea how far she had come or where she was. Her body was colder than she could ever remember it being before, only her fingers and toes relieved of the stinging pain which afflicted the rest of her. The wind sliced through her jacket, driving the snow into her face. Everywhere she turned there was only snow and more snow. She took a tentative step, felt her ankle give way and fell waist-deep into a massive drift. Fear overwhelmed her. She was lost in a raging blizzard with no hope of finding her way back to the house. Too late she recalled macabre tales of people wandering round in circles until they dropped dead of fatigue and cold. She couldn't have come very far, she told herself. All she had to do was to retrace her footsteps, but when she turned the snow had already obliterated them. Silently she prayed for the wind to drop so that she could see through the blinding snowstorm, but her prayers went unheeeded.

How could she have been so stupid as to run so heedlessly out of the house? Now with her life at stake her earlier fears seemed trivial, and there was nowhere she would rather have been than wrapped in the secure warmth of Slade's arms.

Secure! She smothered a half-hysterical laugh. There was no security for her with Slade Ashford. But there was life, she thought yearningly, and a depth of passion that promised to hold a special magic of its own.

She shivered again, cold to the bone, and pulled off a glove to wipe the snow out of her eyes. Her fingers looked oddly white and felt curiously lifeless. Fear lurched in her stomach as she recalled reading about the dangers of frostbite. But this was England, she reminded herself. She couldn't die less than fifteen miles from civilisation—it just wasn't possible.

But she knew that it was. Desperation lent her the strength to take a few more tentative steps before she lost her footing and plunged full length into a deep bank of snow. Fear swamped her, weak tears of despair trickling damply down her cold face. Then a sound that was not simply the harsh keening of the wind seemed to reach her, and she strained to catch it.

Hope flared inside her—Slade must have come after her. Struggling to get to her feet, she found to her horror that her right ankle wouldn't support her.

'Slade!' She called his name until her throat was hoarse, unable to believe she simply hadn't called him up out of her imagination when he suddenly materialised at her side, the shoulders of the heavy dark jacket he wore thickly powdered with snow.

'Oh, Slade, thank God!' Chelsea was crying and

laughing at the same time, not caring what she betrayed in her relief at seeing him.

Even his rough, 'You crazy fool, what the hell do you think you're doing?' didn't have the power to frighten her.

'Where are we?' she asked him when he reached her. 'I'm completely lost.'

'About a mile from the house,' he told her curtly. 'And next time you decide to pull a stunt like this you might at least wait until I'm adequately dressed for it. Come on.' He leaned down to help her out of the drift, frowning when he felt her body sag. 'What's the matter?'

'It's my ankle,' Chelsea admitted ruefully. 'I've twisted it, I think. It keeps giving way every time I try to put any weight on it.'

'That's all we need!' She was caught off guard when Slade bent down and picked her up bodily.

'It's the only way,' he told her harshly. 'Oh, I realise how much you hate the thought of me touching you—you've made that abundantly plain. Didn't it strike you that a simple "no, thanks" might have done just as well?'

'I'd already tried that, remember?' she snapped back at him, wincing as he almost stumbled, jarring her ankle.

'You might have mouthed the words, but there was damn little conviction behind them,' Slade claimed. 'Quite the contrary. But you've made your point now all right.'

There was an odd inflection to his voice that might almost have been pain, but Chelsea told herself that she was letting her imagination run away with her.

'Didn't it occur to you, the danger you were risking?' he demanded bitterly. 'Running out like that with nothing for protection but a thin coat and a pair of fashion boots?'

His scorn scorched her already tender nerves.

'I just wanted to escape,' she murmured painfully, without adding that her flight had been from her own emotions as much as from him.

'Thanks a million. You do wonders for my ego!' He paused, bracing himself to support her weight, breathing deeply, and Chelsea felt ashamed of goading him when he was risking his own life to save hers.

'I'm sorry,' she whispered huskily. 'I didn't think. I meant to go to Darkwater, but somehow I lost my way and ...'

His savage, 'You're damned lucky you didn't lose your life as well!' cut across her apology, and his mouth was grim with anger as he trudged through the steadily deepening snow. 'You realise that even someone who knows these hills like the back of their hands wouldn't risk going out in a blizzard like this? Familiar landmarks can be wiped out faster than you can turn round. It's a mercy you hadn't gone any farther.'

'I stopped when I couldn't see the elms any longer,' Chelsea admitted. 'I was terrified, and so cold—I just couldn't feel my fingers and toes.'

Slade came to an abrupt halt. 'Can you feel them now?' he demanded, watching her.

Chelsea shook her head slowly, fear spiralling up inside her, not needing to ask why Slade suddenly increased his pace to a degree which she knew must be punishing.

The snowy shape of the Dower House suddenly materialising out of the blizzard was the most welcome sight she had ever seen. Slade carried her into the study, disregarding her protests about their snow-covered clothes and the resultant damp puddles, simply reaching for the phone.

Chelsea heard him swear.

'Out of order,' he said heavily when she looked enquiringly at him. She had been trying to remove her boots with her strangely white hands, but they simply refused to move. 'Let me look.'

She flinched as he examined the dead white flesh, his face darkening.

He flung out of the study, returning within seconds carrying a bottle and a glass.

'Drink it,' he urged her when he had poured a large measure. 'It will help, in more than one way,' he added under his breath as she dutifully drained the dark amber liquid.

Fire burned its way down to her stomach, followed by a delicious warmth.

'Brandy,' Slade told her briefly. 'Unfortunately we've yet to train our sheepdogs to carry it to snow-beleaguered tourists. Now just sit there while I get those boots off.'

He didn't waste time on the zips, and Chelsea winced as he cut through the expensive leather with a knife he had brought from the kitchen.

'I don't believe this,' he said softly when he had cut away her jeans to reveal the smooth flesh of her leg. 'Surely common sense warned you to wear some additional form of protection, such as socks?'

'There wasn't room,' Chelsea admitted feebly. She had contemplated wearing a pair of thick socks she had brought with her, but when she put them on it had been impossible to zip up her boots.

She winced as Slade started to rub life into her numbed feet. Her toes remained completely unfeeling, but her ankle were she had turned on it was throbbing painfully.

'By rights you should see a doctor,' Slade told her, 'but seeing that we're unable to summon one right now, you'll just have to force yourself to suffer my ministrations. Of course,' he added suavely, 'I could always leave you to your fate; I might almost be doing myself a favour if I did,' he added under his breath, as he bent to lift her out of the chair.

The brandy had made her feel muzzy and lightheaded, and it seemed too much of an effort to protest when Slade carried her into his room instead of her own. Even the sure touch of his fingers on her clothes failed to awaken any instinct for self-preservation. Her eyelids felt curiously heavy and she kept longing to close them, but every time she slid towards unconsciousness Slade shook her.

Every bit of her body apart from her fingers and toes ached. She watched Slade examining them with detached interest, aware with a careless floating indifference that he was frowning.

'Can you feel that?'

She shook her head as he touched her toes, wondering at the expression of grim determination in his eyes.

He also examined her swollen ankle. 'I don't think it's broken, more likely sprained.'

Chelsea shivered, suddenly terribly cold, an odd nausea rising up inside her. She managed to quell it, but nothing seemed to be able to stop the increasingly violent tremors gripping her. She tried to sit up and was instantly overwhelmed by a terrifying dizziness.

'Lie down,' Slade cautioned her, and disappeared in the direction of the bathroom.

Chelsea could hear the sound of running water, and when he returned his sweater had been discarded, his shirt sleeves rolled up to the elbow.

'Chelsea!' She responded instinctively to the incisive note of command in his voice. 'If we don't do something about these,' he tapped her feet briefly, 'you could be in real danger from frostbite. We can do two things—wait and hope that circulation will return as your body heat builds up, or try to speed matters up a little.'

Chelsea grimaced. The brandy he had given her was making her feel decidedly odd, and yet curiously not even the gravity of what he had told her seemed to have much power to affect her.

'What do you want me to do?' she demanded. 'Sit with my feet in a bowl of boiling water?'

'Something like that.' He was bending over her, reaching for the buttons on her blouse. She drew back instinctively, her eyes widening.

'Look——' impatience and something else lurked in the depths of his eyes, 'I'm not about to rape you. Hot water merely on your feet isn't enough. I've run a bath for you and you'll stay in it until your hands and feet tingle and smart with returning circulation. Is that clear?'

All too clear. His words had penetrated the

comfortable brandy-induced fog which had en-
shrouded her, and Chelsea sat up to protest.

'Drink this.' Slade produced another glass of
brandy. 'Drink it, Chelsea,' he warned her,
'otherwise I'll pour it down your throat.'

Unwillingly she did so, telling him huskily that
she could manage without his unwanted ministrations, her face burning at the thought of his hands
on her body.

'Oh, of course you can,' he agreed sardonically.
'It's a very minor task to get from here to the
bathroom with one ankle out of action and both
feet so numb that you can hardly stand up on
them. I've already told you,' he reiterated
impatiently, 'as far as I'm concerned you're
completely safe. Somehow the fact that you'd
rather face a raging blizzard than my obviously
unwelcome advances has had a decidedly cooling
effect on my ardour.'

Her initial feeling was one of intense disappointment, but the brandy was having its effect upon
her. Chelsea seldom drank more than the
occasional glass of wine, and the potency of the
spirit on an empty stomach was acting like a
tranquiliser on her overwrought mind, forcing it
into a state of hazy lethargy.

This time when Slade deftly unfastened her
buttons she made not the slightest protest,
allowing him to completely remove her blouse
without demur. The remnants of her jeans quickly
followed, and although she knew she should be
embarrassed when he bent swiftly to remove her
bra and briefs she was hazily conscious only of a
surging pleasure engendered by the briefly acci-

dental brush of his fingers against the smooth curve of her breast. For a second he seemed to stiffen into rigidity, but Chelsea barely had time to register the fact before he was lifting her up in his arms and carrying her towards the elegantly male bathroom decorated in dark blues and gold.

CHAPTER EIGHT

She hadn't realised just how cold she was until she felt the blissfully warm lap of the water against her skin, Chelsea acknowledged dreamily, flinching as Slade tapped her lightly on the cheek and said curtly, 'Don't go to sleep on me, Chelsea. I want to know the moment you feel life coming back to your feet.'

He was more concerned with her feet than she was, Chelsea reflected, for some reason finding the knowledge amusing. She wanted to laugh so much her laughter was like a tight bubble inside her, but something warned her that Slade would be angry if she did. She also wanted to luxuriate in the delicious warmth of the water, to lie down in it and let it lap over her while she drifted off to sleep.

'Chelsea!'

She yelped as Slade turned on the tap and hot water gushed into the dark blue depths of the bath.

'I want to go to sleep,' she protested childishly, smothering a yawn, and frowning a little as she heard Slade swear. He seemed very angry about something, but somehow it was just too much of an effort to work out why.

'Your feet . . . can you feel them yet?'

Giggling, Chelsea reached down and touched her toes. 'I think so—are these them?'

She thought she heard Slade mutter something uncomplimentary under his breath, coupled with something about 'too much damned brandy', but it didn't really register. All of a sudden she felt gloriously free of inhibition and caution. What did she need them for? she asked recklessly, watching Slade through downcast lashes, wondering what he would say if she suggested that he join her. The bath was after all large enough for both of them.

She frowned as pain suddenly lanced through her ankle combined with red-hot darts of fire in her toes, gasping as the pain increased in severity, and all the colour left her face.

Slade was cruelly unsympathetic, his muttered 'thank God!' filling her with irrational resentment. Instead of comforting her as she wanted him to do he seemed to take great pleasure in increasing her discomfort by roughly massaging the flesh of her feet. To punish him she withdrew her foot from his grasp, splashing him deliberately as he reached out to recapture it. Water soaked the front of his shirt and she giggled helplessly.

'You're drunk.'

'Am I?' she smiled sweetly up at him, not really caring if it was the truth or not, her eyes rounding provocatively as she said huskily, 'Whose fault's that?'

'Look . . .' He grimaced suddenly, then reached down to lift her out of the water, not seeming to care that she was soaking the front of his shirt and jeans. Chelsea didn't care either. It was blissfully satisfying to be held against him like this, the brandy obligingly releasing her hold on reality so completely that it was impossible for her to think beyond the immediate present.

She pouted when Slade wrapped her in a thick towel, but the feel of his hands on her body as he briskly rubbed her dry was so delicious that she soon forgot the disappointment of being removed from the close contact of his body.

'Bed for you,' he told her grittily when he had finished. 'Something tells me you're going to have an almighty hangover in the morning. Are you hungry?'

Chelsea shook her head, closing her eyes as he picked her up and walked into the bedroom. He had reached the door before she realised where he was taking her.

'No!' she protested as he reached for the handle. 'I want to stay here.' Dimly she realised that she was flirting with potential dynamite, but suddenly it didn't seem at all important; other and more urgent desires clamoured for utterance.

With a faint grimace Slade walked across to his own bed, thrusting aside the covers and sliding her inside, before securing them round her as firmly as though she were a child.

In drowsy satisfaction Chelsea watched him remove his soaking shirt and jeans, her heart thudding painfully as she studied the clean lines of his body clad only in briefs which did little to disguise his masculinity. As she watched him she started to tremble feverishly with the longing to feel his hard warmth against her, her whole body shaking with the need she had dammed up for so long. Slade removed a clean shirt from a drawer and started to fasten the buttons. Chelsea's skin felt clammy and she was dreadfully cold. He had found a clean pair of jeans and was pulling them on. She tried to tell him how terribly cold she was and how much she wished she was back in the languorous warmth of the bathroom.

Tucking his shirt into his jeans, Slade walked across to the bed to study her dispassionately, and Chelsea thought she heard him mutter under his breath, 'This is all I need,' but she couldn't be absolutely sure because her mind seemed to be playing tricks on her, making the room recede, strangely out of focus and making her feel as cold as though she were still out in the snow when in reality she ought to be lovely and warm.

'Slade.' Her small whisper checked him. She wished he didn't always frown when she spoke to him, Chelsea thought unhappily, watching the telltale gesture. 'Slade, I'm dreadfully cold,' she told him, her teeth starting to chatter. 'I feel cold right through inside and out, even though I can feel my toes.'

'Chelsea——' he began warningly, but her teeth were chattering so loudly that he had no need to touch her ice-cold skin to know she was telling the truth. 'Slade, I'm freezing—please help me get warm,' she pleaded huskily.

There was a long silence when she wondered hazily what she had said now to anger him. She looked hesitantly up at him, dismayed by the fixed rigidity of his expression and the small pulse beating tensely in his jaw.

'Slade!'

'I heard you,' he answered grimly. 'You really believe in turning the screws, don't you?' he added bitterly, but Chelsea was feeling too hazy to know what he meant. All she did know was that she longed for the male warmth of his body against the icy coldness of hers, and she couldn't seem to make him understand.

For a moment she thought he was going to walk away and leave her, and she started to tremble, violently overcome by another icy shivering fit, but when she opened her eyes he had already removed his shirt and his hands were on the buckle of his belt, and she felt her tension ease enough for the violence of her shudders to ease a little.

When he slid into the bed beside her she curled up against him like a small kitten seeking warmth, almost ready to purr with pleasure when his arms reached out to hold her.

Just for a moment he seemed to tense and draw away, but sleep was already claiming Chelsea, drawing her down into an embrace almost as warm and comforting as Slade's.

At her side Slade remained awake, an expression on his face which suggested that neither Chelsea's presence nor his own thoughts brought any surcease to whatever had drawn the tight lines of pain beside his mouth.

Chelsea was dreaming. She was lost in a whirling demoniacal snowstorm, battling against the biting intensity of a wind which seemed intent on stripping the flesh from her bones, pursuing her relentlessly no matter how she tried to escape from it. She moaned in her sleep, moving restlessly, and the hand she had raised to ward off the cold suddenly came into contact with the solid warmth of Slade's chest.

She awoke immediately, disorientated and bewildered, unable to understand where she was or with whom, and then as her eyes searched the unfamiliar darkness of Slade's bedroom everything came rushing back; at least up until the moment when Slade had made her drink the brandy. After that events took on a hazy quality as though they were something she had seen on a screen rather than participated in; no, not merely participated in, she acknowledged grimly, remembering how she had begged Slade to stay with her, but actively initiated.

Slade! She risked a look at him. He was lying on his side facing her, his eyes closed. In sleep he looked less austere and more vulnerable. Without thinking she reached out to brush the thick dark hair off his forehead. Beneath her fingertips his skin felt vibrantly warm and alive. She remembered how cold she had been and how it had felt to be held in his arms. She also remembered how annoyed he had been, and vividly remembered him saying that she was safe from him now. She knew she ought to be relieved; that was after all what she had wanted, but instead she found herself having to stifle a swift stab of disappointment.

Her head ached—an aftermath of the brandy she had drunk, she reflected, then she suddenly remembered her ankle and moved her foot experimentally to see if it still hurt.

There was pain, but it was minimal. Chelsea lowered her foot, freezing instinctively as it brushed against Slade's calf, and the realisation came to her that beneath the protective bedclothes they were both naked.

A longing to be close to Slade overwhelmed her, flooding her with what her brain told her was a crazily impulsive need which she would be wiser to fight against than give in to, and whether it was because enough of last night's brandy still lingered in her veins to override habitual caution and wariness or not, Chelsea didn't know, but it seemed impossible to prevent herself from moving closer to Slade's unmoving form and almost exult in the throwing off of years of self-repression.

Once that barrier was breached it seemed the most natural thing in the world for her to reach out experimentally to touch the dark shadow along Slade's jaw with fingertips acutely sensitised to the rough texture of overnight beard, thrilling to the knowledge that there was something acutely erotic in so doing.

With new honesty she admitted that she wanted Slade's possession of her body, even if it was without love. Pain filled her. Part of her mind told her that she should have more pride, but that other new Chelsea argued fiercely that surely she had the right to this; to give herself freely to the only man she was ever likely to love?

Her fingers stilled and she raised herself slightly to look down into his face, studying it avidly. In repose there was a slight curl to his mouth, hinting at a sense of humour. Thick black lashes protected her from the sharp intensity of his eyes. He moved suddenly and the sheet slipped down between them. Her skin looked pale against his tanned flesh, Chelsea noted, and lifted her fingers to touch the smooth column of this throat. He was oblivious to her tentative caress and it gave her the courage to bend her head and lightly touch her lips to his skin. It was warm and faintly salty and felt so pleasurable beneath the hesitant exploration of her mouth that all thought of any possible danger slid from her mind. Totally engrossed in her tactile voyage of discovery, Chelsea was oblivious to everything but the scent and taste of Slade's body, the hunger she had dammed up from the first time she met him spilling over to close her mind and her senses to everything but the feel of his skin beneath her hands and lips.

Her tongue was tracing a delicate path along the brown shoulder closest to her when she suddenly became aware that something had changed; the change was so subtle that it was several seconds before she realised what had happened, some sixth sense relaying to her the fact that the smooth skin beneath her hand was no longer inanimate, but seemed to be radiating a sensual responsiveness which set alarm bells ringing long enough for her to raise her head and encounter Slade's slumberously aroused green gaze.

His hand reached out to capture the length of her hair and hold her against him, his voice husky and warm as he murmured, 'What exactly are you trying to do? Take advantage of a poor helpless male?'

Heat scorched her skin, the shock of finding him awake arousing all her own instinctive fears, but it was too late to move away. With one lazy movement Slade turned towards her, imprisoning her in his arms and trapping her beneath him with the weight of his body. At the first touch of his skin against hers, Chelsea's resistance melted. This was what she wanted; what she craved for; what she had been born for. Feverish tremors shivered through her, punctuated by delicate shudders of pleasure as Slade bent his head and traced a sensuous pathway over her shoulders and throat, pausing a mere breath away from her lips. His fingers stroked caressingly over her shoulders and Chelsea felt as though she were drowning in the pleasure of his touch. Her hands reached upwards, entwining in the dark thickness of his hair, impelling him to close the tiny distance between them, but Slade resisted her, his palms flat on the bed either side of her head as he studied her minutely.

Chelsea no longer cared what he read in her face or in the hurried rise and fall of her breathing.

'Slade!'

His name was a plea and both of them knew it. His hands left the bed to frame her face, his eyes searching every feature, and then as though satisfied with what he saw he bent his head, lightly brushing her lips with his.

Her blood turned to liquid fire, Chelsea strained upwards, hungry for more than light teasing kisses, sensing instinctively that Slade was deliberately holding himself in check; waiting for her total self-abasement and capitulation, a tiny voice warned her, but she ignored it.

'Slade?'

This time her husky plea was answered, with the hot pressure of his mouth and a passion no longer leashed, but smothering her in velvet black darkness, awakening her to sensations she had never dreamed existed, drawing from her a felinely sensuous response she had never known she possessed, glorying in the knowledge that Slade was no longer master of his desire for her, his caresses increasingly urgent as he thrust aside the sheet and bent his head to place the burning heat of his mouth against the exposed curves of her breasts.

Her heart was beating so heavily she half expected it to burst the wall of her ribs. A hectic flush stained Slade's skin, his eyes so dark that they were almost black, his arousal obvious, and yet it seemed to Chelsea that he was intent only on increasing her pleasure rather than satisfying his desire, and she knew instinctively that whatever else she might regret her body would always remember these moments with intense pleasure.

Slade was a skilled lover; Chelsea closed her mind to how he had obtained those skills, shivering ecstatically as his hands moved delicately over her body, tracing the shape of her spine and the narrow curve of her waist before stroking softly over her hips and the slender curve of her thighs, his touch turning her boneless with pleasure, as supple and sensual as a small cat in his arms, delighting in his exploration of her body and the knowledge that touching her aroused him.

His tongue traced circles around her nipples, witnessing their response and encouraging it in a manner that made her gasp and twist into his arms, pressing passionate kisses against his skin, recklessly uncaring of what she was betraying.

She heard Slade groan and cried out in protest as his mouth touched demandingly against the quivering flesh of her stomach, his hands soothing her minute tremors but increasing the gnawing ache deep down inside her.

Her own hands reached instinctively to caress the taut maleness of Slade's hips, teasing the vulnerability of the smooth flatness of his stomach before tracing the dark arrowing of body hair downwards until he trembled and groaned, his response fuelling her own intense desire until her bones ached with the need for fulfilment.

His mouth felt hot as he buried it in her throat, a wild pulse beating under the fingertips she stroked against his flesh.

'Has any other man made you feel like this?' he demanded huskily, lifting his head and studying the aroused pleasure in her face. 'Has he?' he repeated forcefully, anger mingling with passion, and with a jolting sickness Chelsea felt herself come back to earth. She started to shiver with reaction, sickened both by her own behaviour and Slade's egotistical desire to arouse within her something she had felt for no one else.

Stifling her emotions, she forced herself to go rigid in his arms, noting with satisfaction the darkening in his eyes as he felt her reaction. In the space of a few seconds they had gone from lovers to enemies, each ready to use every weapon at their command to wound the other. At least he had not realised that she loved him, Chelsea thought in relief; possibly because love as a viable emotion would simply never occur to a man who merely experienced physical lust.

'What's wrong?' she goaded. 'Are you wondering how you compare? Would you like a rating on a scale of one to ten?'

For a moment she thought he was going to hit her, but with a tremendous effort of will he seemed to gain control of himself, desire converted into blazing anger as he stared contemptuously down into her face.

'You're an extremely desirable and sexy woman, as I'm sure you already know, but all of a sudden the only feeling you arouse in me is one of nausea, combined with a need to wash the taint of you off my body!'

He pushed aside the bedclothes and swung his feet to the floor, leaving Chelsea to stare in sick shock after him as he disappeared into the bathroom. How long she lay trying to come to terms with the pain of the wounds he had just inflicted she didn't know, but at last she managed to find the strength to limp into her own room, still shaking with reaction and self-disgust. As she opened her door she caught sight of her reflection in the mirror. Her eyes looked too large for her over-pale face, lilac smudges lay like bruises against her skin, and a raw agony in her expression gave away the truth.

She badly wanted the relief of tears, but she couldn't cry. All her emotions seemed to be locked up inside her as the traumatic aftermath of her own behaviour swept over her. She shuddered violently as she relived how she had felt; how she had touched and actively encouraged Slade, almost unable to believe that she was reliving the actions of herself and not a stranger.

She glanced out of the window and saw the silver glint of moonlight on the snow. A closer look confirmed that the blizzard had stopped, but the snow lay thick and deep. She shivered, creeping into her cold bed and pulling the blankets up around her, wishing that she could simply find oblivion in sleep and not wake up until the snow had gone and with it Slade Ashford.

It didn't help knowing that she had no one but herself to blame—herself and possibly the brandy, she thought grimly, recalling how the fierce spirit had undermined her defences to the extent where she was no longer prepared to listen to the voice of caution. How could she have been so stupid? She thumped her pillow despairingly. She had known how Slade felt about her; how determined he had been to salve his ego—and what had she done? Ignored all the promptings of caution and common sense and stupidly given him the means to hurt her.

At least he hadn't guessed the truth, she comforted herself; but no thanks to her. If he hadn't spoken as he had at this very moment she could have been lying in his arms trying to work out how to explain away the fact that she had still been a virgin.

Infuriatingly, although with Darren she had been fiercely glad of the fact that she had not succumbed to him, her feelings towards Slade were still ambivalent. Her brain told her that she had had a lucky escape, but her body still yearned for him.

It was dawn before she slept, only to be awakened abruptly by the sound of activity outside the house.

Her first thought was—how on earth was she to

face Slade? Unless she had been mistaken about the conditions outside there was no way they would be able to get away from the house. She frowned, realising that by now Slade should have been in New York. Her initial thought when she had returned yesterday and seen him had been that he had deliberately lied to her about leaving, but now she recognised that he was hardly likely to have indulged in such an elaborate deception simply to be alone with her. So what had happened?

She was hardly likely to find out, she reflected, as she pulled on her robe and padded over to the window.

Outside the sky was a pure pale blue. Frost sparkled crisply on the snow, a pale lemon sun struggling to add an illusion of warmth to the winter scene. Down below Chelsea saw Slade trudging back from the garage. Despite the icy cold as evidenced by his breath, he was bareheaded, his boots leaving deep tracks in the thick snow. He paused suddenly and glanced upwards, causing Chelsea to duck away from the window, not wanting him to see her.

Limping into her bathroom, she examined herself. Apart from a slightly swollen ankle she seemed to have suffered remarkably few after-effects from her exposure. Mainly thanks to Slade, she was forced to acknowledge, a hazy recollection of hot water and her own protests surfacing briefly.

How long would it be before the snow melted? She dressed quickly in cords and a thick sweater. The central heating appeared to be on, but she had no idea how reliable it would be under the present conditions.

In the kitchen she busied herself preparing breakfast. It was apparent from the clinical tidiness that Slade had not eaten, and telling herself that there was nothing to be gained from exacerbating their position, Chelsea opened the fridge and removed several rashers of the bacon Mrs Rudge always served him for breakfast, and several eggs.

He came in as she was filling the kettle, and stopped on the threshold, obviously surprised to see her up.

'I'm just making breakfast,' she told him calmly, glad that the necessity of filling the kettle meant that she could keep her back to him. 'It won't be long.'

He made no comment and for a moment Chelsea thought he was simply going to ignore her, but when she eventually turned round he was removing his boots and then he went across to fiddle with the radio on top of one of the units.

'Might as well hear the weather forecast,' he told her, 'although I don't suppose it will be good. There was a sharp frost last night—I thought we might be able to get the car out, but there's simply no way.'

'At least we're warm and comfortable,' Chelsea murmured, avoiding his eyes, her skin flushing as she recalled just how warm and comfortable she had felt in the night, sharing his bed.

She had always enjoyed cooking and moved deftly in the immaculate kitchen. There was a strange expression in Slade's eyes when she

eventually placed his breakfast in front of him,
which deepened when he took a tentative bite and
pronounced as though it surprised him, 'It's good!'

Chelsea said nothing, simply pouring him the
cup of tea she knew he preferred in the morning.

'But of course I suppose breakfasts are your
forte,' he said smoothly when she didn't speak.
'You've probably had a lot of practice at making
them.'

Typical of a man! she thought wrathfully as she
turned away. It was all right for them to be
sexually experienced and liberated, but when it
was a woman they were full of outraged masculine
pride and nasty innuendoes.

'What business is it of yours if I have?' she
demanded sweetly, 'You're enjoying the results,
aren't you?'

With an abruptness that startled her he pushed
his half eaten breakfast away.

'I was,' he agreed bitingly, 'but suddenly I've
lost the taste for it. I'm going to my study—to
work,' he added as though underlining that he
wanted to keep away from her.

He was gone before Chelsea had any opportunity
to ask him why he hadn't gone to New York as he
had planned. Tomorrow was Christmas Day, she
realised with a start, suddenly overwhelmed by
loneliness and a longing to be with her family.

It was very tempting to pick up the phone and
ring Ann, but she daren't trust herself not to betray
to her sister that something was wrong, and it
would be both selfish and unfair to spoil things for
her, simply because she was suffering from a bout
of homesickness.

But it wasn't simply 'homesickness', she acknowledged as she rescued what she could of Slade's breakfast for the birds and started to wash up; there was heartsickness as well, and that couldn't be as easily assuaged.

Her head started to ache during the morning, and by mid-afternoon her whole body seemed to be one aching, shivering mass. It didn't need Slade's curt pronouncement over dinner to tell her what was wrong with her and she prayed that all she had was simply a bad cold and not the beginnings of 'flu.

She didn't think she could remember a more dismal Christmas, Chelsea reflected the following morning as she sneezed and shivered her way downstairs, and that included the year her parents had died. At least then there had been Ann, who had tried to make something of the day for her younger sister.

She couldn't face breakfast; there was no sign of Slade apart from the crockery draining by the sink. He was obviously up and had eaten—another sign that her company was neither required nor needed? she wondered wryly, wondering why the knowledge should cause her so much pain when she already knew in full depth his contempt for her.

Dinner the previous night had been a nightmare of cold silence punctuated by her own stilted attempts at conversation. Apart from warning her that she was not well, Slade had said nothing. He hadn't looked particularly healthy himself, Chelsea remembered. There had been a tension about him that was unusual; a set expression in his eyes which had said very loudly and plainly 'Keep out.'

She was dosing herself with some cold remedy she had found in the medicine cabinet when she first became aware of the sound of an engine. At first she thought that Slade had actually started the car, even though common sense told her that he wouldn't get very far in it, but it was a battered Land Rover that materialised out of the snowy lane, chugging determinedly towards them.

Forgetting her mental vow not to address Slade again until he spoke to her, Chelsea ran into the study, calling out to him, but Slade was already standing by the window watching the progress of the Land Rover.

When it came to a standstill and Tom's burly figure climbed out Chelsea bit her lip, remembering their last meeting.

'Cavalry to the rescue,' Slade said sardonically. 'Something tells me he's going to have a shock when he discovers I'm here with you.'

If he was shocked, Tom hid it very well. His smile for Chelsea was as it had been when they first met, friendly and open, just a tinge of embarrassment in his eyes as they met hers.

To Chelsea's surprise he wasn't alone in the Land Rover. Sandy was with him.

'Ma insisted we come down to make sure you were all right,' he explained.

Chelsea sneezed, and instantly Sandy was all professional, frowning and reaching for her wrist to take her pulse.

'You've got 'flu,' she pronounced unnecessarily when they were back in the house. 'You should be in bed.'

'Exactly what I told her,' Slade commented dryly, watching the colour run up under Chelsea's skin with clinical detachment.

'Come back to the farm with us,' Tom suggested. 'Ma will look after you.'

It was a tempting prospect. Sandy's hand on her forehead felt beautifully cool. Her head seemed to be stuffed with a peculiar form of cotton wool that felt as heavy as lead, and she could think of nothing better that being coddled by Mrs Little. She opened her eyes and saw that Sandy's were focused on her with narrowed wariness. Poor girl, she was probably out of her mind with jealousy because Chelsea had been alone with Slade.

She opened her mouth to accept Tom's offer, but instead heard Slade saying coolly, 'Oh, there's no need for that. I'm sure your mother already has enough on her hands, Tom. I think I'm perfectly capable of nursemaiding a 'flu victim.'

'Slade's right,' Sandy confirmed to Chelsea's further amazement. 'I've got my bag with me and there are some antibiotics in it which I can give you. They should help speed things up. If you want me you can always phone. I'm staying up at the farm to give Val and Dad a chance to have Christmas alone with the twins.'

'If you want to drive us back I can loan you the Land Rover,' Tom suggested to Slade. 'It's pretty ancient and we only use it in bad weather, but we can always manage with the Range Rover until this stuff clears. Fortunately we were all prepared for it, so we shouldn't lose any stock.'

Slade accepted, and when the three of them had gone, Chelsea dragged herself up to her room,

Sandy's instructions ringing in her ears.

She was asleep when Slade came back, and returned to consciousness groggily to discover him standing over her bed, one cool hand against her flushed face.

'How are you feeling?'

'Hot and aching,' Chelsea admitted, 'and thirsty.'

'The last problem's easily remedied. Mrs Little has sent you some of her homemade barley water. Apparently it works wonders. I'll go and get you a glass.'

If he wasn't sympathetic at least he wasn't as cold and remote as he had been, Chelsea reflected achingly when Slade had gone. Her sheets seemed to be full of tiny gritty objects which dug into her tender skin, and her whole body seemed to ache with a nagging pain which even affected her bones.

When Slade returned she was shivering convulsively, although she tried to hide it from him. Having him towering over her while she lay in bed made her feel distinctly at a disadvantage.

'Sit up and drink this.'

Like a small child she did as she was told, puzzled when Slade disappeared into her bathroom, only to return within seconds with her sponge and a towel.

'Sandy said this would help you to feel cooler,' he said dispassionately as he pushed the straps of her nightdress off her shoulders and sponged her burning skin with cool detachment. If he expected her to feel grateful to him he could think again, Chelsea decided crossly when her broderie anglaise straps were once again in place.

'I could have done that myself,' she snapped childishly, 'but I suppose it gives you some sense of power to treat me like a child!'

His mouth compressed in a grim line, his eyes as unfathomable and unfeeling as jade as he retorted in a clipped voice, 'I'm trying very hard to remind myself that you're not well. Now, Mrs Little suggested an omelette for your supper—I know it isn't turkey . . .' Chelsea felt nauseated at the thought of any rich food, and ashamed of goading him. If it wasn't for her Slade could have spent Christmas up at the farm with Sandy to adore him.

'I suppose Sandy would have preferred you to stay up there,' she said jealously.

He had turned away from her and paused, eyebrows rising. 'Why should she—she's got what she wants. Tom,' he enlightened, when she looked blank. 'Surely you must have realised that she's in love with him?'

'Sandy loves Tom?'

Slade's gaze sharpened. 'You know she does, we've already discussed it once.'

Chelsea mumbled an assent, unwilling to admit to him that she had believed the other girl to be in love with him. So that was why Sandy had looked so rigidly at her before, and perhaps why she had suggested that Slade should nurse her down here. She ought to have realised; no sane woman urges the man she loves to stay alone with a potential rival.

'And Tom?'

'Worried by the thought of losing an admirer?' he drawled. 'Tom was dazzled by you, but at heart he's a man who knows sterling worth when he sees it, and old-fashioned enough to expect virtue and loyalty in his wife.'

'Would you?'

For a long moment there was silence, and then with a sigh he straightened up to face her.

'I hope I'm not hypocritical enough to expect an innocence in another that I no longer have any claim to myself, but yes, I would want and look for sexual fidelity for the future; and a love deep enough to match my own.'

'Love?' Chelsea's voice trembled on the word, a funny little pain aching inside her. 'You surprise me, I didn't think you believed in such an emotion.'

'I don't necessarily believe in an after-life, but that doesn't stop me from illogically hoping it's there,' he told her enigmatically.

CHAPTER NINE

IT was almost New Year before Chelsea was well enough to get up. Sandy came down to see her twice, and on the second occasion told her that she was now well enough to get up.

'Have you heard that they postponed the Young Farmers' Ball because of the bad weather?' she asked Slade. 'They're holding it tomorrow now, why don't both of you come?'

Chelsea expected Slade to demur, but to her consternation he said evenly, 'Good idea, I think we will.'

'I'll tell Tom to arrange tickets,' Sandy said gaily. 'We can make a foursome.'

When she had gone Chelsea said shakily, 'I'm not going to that ball, I can't . . .'

'You haven't anything to wear,' Slade finished mockingly for her.

It wasn't what she had been going to say, but she coloured to the roots of her hair, remembering the scene with Tom.

'I'm not wearing that dress,' she said flatly, shuddering at the thought of it, 'and nothing you can say will make me change my mind.'

'Nothing I can say,' Slade agreed evenly, 'but plenty I can do. We're going, Chelsea; and you're going to wear that dress. You owe it to Sandy if nothing else. One look at you in that will convince Tom more than a thousand words that you simply aren't the woman for him.'

'No? Who am I the woman for, then?' she challenged recklessly, tears burning the back of her throat. 'You?'

'Me, and any other man willing to pay the price,' he taunted cruelly. 'But Tom isn't like that. He wants marriage and permanency—plus a commitment we both know that you're incapable of giving.'

The fates all seemed to conspire against her, ably aided by Slade, Chelsea decided darkly when Tom telephoned with the information that he had been able to secure tickets for them. It was in vain for her to protest that she did not want to go; she would go if he had to drag her there, Slade informed her unkindly, adding that she could look upon it as a form of repayment to Sandy for her

ministrations to her. It was on the tip of her
tongue to point out that his ministrations had been
far more intimate than Sandy's and to demand
what form of payment he was going to seek, but
just in time she stopped herself. She had enough
self-knowledge to know that if he chose to look
upon her words as a sexual challenge she wouldn't
be able to resist him.

It seemed that the Ball was something eagerly
anticipated locally. The snow had cleared
sufficiently for them to get to and from the
village, although they still had to use the Land
Rover.

Chelsea went up to her room the next morning
after breakfast and discovered that Slade had left
her blue dress on the bed. She looked at it with
revulsion, hating the thought of wearing it. It was
not so much the dress itself, she admitted, but the
memories it evoked. Part of her longed to defy
Slade and tell him that nothing would make her
wear it, but caution prevailed.

The arrangements were that Tom and Sandy
would pick them up in the Range Rover and they
would all travel together. Uncomfortably aware
that she could so easily have been Tom's partner
rather than Slade's, Chelsea wasn't too happy
with the arrangement, although it was infinitely
preferable to being alone with Slade.

Ever since the night she had run away from him
he seemed to have changed; before she had feared
him simply because she didn't think herself
capable of resisting if he chose to seduce her; now
there was a brooding, almost menacing air about
him, coupled with a tense explosiveness which she

found hard to equate with the coolly sardonic man she knew him to be.

Supper was being provided by the hotel, and after a light tea, Chelsea excused herself to go and get ready. She had spent the morning pressing the crumpled ball of silk and now it hung on her wardrobe door, a rich pool of colour against the wood.

On this occasion, since she was not playing a part, there was no need for her to dress as she had done before, and besides, she hadn't brought with her the provocatively feminine underwear she had worn on that occasion.

She was just about to run her bath when her bedroom door was thrust open and Slade walked in. He had spent the morning in Alnwick and Chelsea had been grateful for his absence. It seemed that whenever he was near her she found it difficult to behave or even think rationally, and as always when she saw him her stomach churned with a mixture of anger and desire. For a moment he simply leaned against the door he had closed behind him, tall and sombre in the black jeans and sweater he was wearing. The fine wool fabric stretched tautly over the breadth of his chest and in an effort to avoid his eyes, Chelsea's slid downwards, coming to an abrupt halt on the buckle of his belt.

'Something I thought you might need,' he said laconically at last, throwing the package he was holding in his hands on to the bed. It spilled open, and Chelsea's face went white as she saw the dainty minuscule briefs and matching suspender belt in the same colour as her dress. Toning stockings were with them. The colour which had left her face so precipitously came flooding back in an angry wave. Her voice shook as she demanded huskily, 'You don't imagine I'm going to wear those?'

'Why not? It's nothing very different from what you had on the last time you wore that dress, unless my memory's playing tricks on me, and I'm damn sure it isn't. What's the matter?' he goaded, 'and don't trot out any rubbish about not wearing underwear provided by a man—some man paid before, even if he didn't personally buy it. Or is it just the fact that I paid for it you object to?' he asked with soft savagery. 'Oh no,' he told her as Chelsea turned blindly away, head bowed, 'you don't get to me by doing that. Wear them, Chelsea,' he warned her, 'otherwise I'll damned well dress you in them myself!'

He would as well, she acknowledged, literally shaking with anger and humiliation when the door had closed behind him.

Half an hour later, as she slid on the sheer silky stockings, she shuddered with the knowledge of Slade's victory. The obvious expense and delicacy of the underwear afforded her little pleasure, and she closed her mind against the thought of Slade's lean brown fingers touching the scanty scraps of satin and lace.

The shoes she had worn before were still in Melchester, but she did have a pair of delicate high-heeled mules which she could wear instead. The shaking hand with which she applied her make-up did little to restore her confidence. Her theatrical training made it impossible for her to deliberately inflict an exaggerated or unflattering mask on her face; if anything her eyeshadow was more subtly subdued than it had been on the previous occasion she had worn the silk dress, although basically it was very similar. Her hair she simply coiled into a smooth chignon, which privately she thought a little stark, unaware of the way in which it drew attention to the long sweep of her throat and the pure lines of her face. As she zipped up the dress she studied her reflection in the mirror, startled to see how it transformed her, adding an aura of sophisticated sexuality she hadn't been so aware of before. It was Slade who had opened her eyes to that particular aspect of her nature, she acknowledged wryly, as she dabbed perfume on her wrists.

'I hope you aren't going to stop there,' Slade commented silkily from behind her.

He had entered her room without her being aware of it, and she stared up at him, startled eyes taking in the immaculate fit of evening clothes that drew subtle attention to the wholly male frame they enclosed.

Her perfume was removed from her unresisting fingers as Slade bent on one knee behind her. She froze as she felt his hand grip the smooth flesh just above her knee.

'If I recall,' he said softly, 'the rule is perfume on every pulse point, am I right?'

Chelsea shivered under the light touch of his hand, remembering how she had deliberately scented her skin in the most provocative fashion she could think of.

There was something dangerously volatile about

Slade tonight; something that warned her not to risk provoking an argument in the intimacy of her bedroom. Inwardly raging and frightened, she submitted to the touch of his fingers against her skin as his thumb stroked caressingly over the place where he had applied her perfume; the backs of her knees; her throat, and lastly the place where her dress dipped to expose the curve of her breasts. His thumb seemed to linger longest there and before he finally turned away Chelsea glimpsed an anger smouldering in his eyes that turned her bones to water.

'So,' he murmured when he had finished, 'now you're exactly as you were the night we met.'

His words struck a chill of warning through Chelsea, panic fluttering wildly through her. What did he mean? Why should he want her to be as she had been when he first met her? Unless . . . Her breath caught in her throat. Was he perhaps regretting allowing his contempt for her to overcome his desire for revenge? Had he decided after all to take what he so arrogantly claimed she owed him?

'Ready?'

His voice was as smooth and bland as velvet. She must have been imagining the anger she had seen in his eyes, Chelsea told herself, because it certainly wasn't there now.

Her only coat was her cream wool one, and she shivered as Slade held it for her while she slid it on. The scent of her own perfume clung almost suffocatingly to her skin and she was aware of an urgent need to escape from the close confines of the house and Slade's presence.

Tom and Sandy arrived on time. Tom looked attractive but slightly uncomfortable in his formal clothes. Sandy was wearing an attractive dress which she confided was a Christmas present from her father.

'But nothing like as fantastic as yours,' she said regretfully, eyeing Chelsea's blue silk. 'It's lovely, isn't it, Tom?'

Chelsea held her breath as Tom glanced at her. There was recognition, and resignation in the look he gave her. 'It's very nice,' he said quietly, reaching across to squeeze Sandy's hand as he added softly, 'But too sophisticated for a baby like you.'

Tears stung the back of Chelsea's throat. Tom couldn't have made it clearer what he thought about her, but she acknowledged that what really hurt was the sardonic smile in Slade's eyes as he watched him. He had been right, she thought tiredly, even if she hadn't fallen in love with Slade, she could never have made Tom happy; not in the way that Sandy probably would.

The hotel where the Ball was to be held was several miles outside the village and had once been a private house. Discreetly extended at the rear to provide a conference centre and additional bedrooms, the hotel was in private ownership and had an ambience that suggested to Chelsea that it could easily rival any one of London's top hotels.

The ballroom was in actual fact the original ballroom of the eighteenth-century mansion, Sandy told her enthusiastically when they were together in the ladies' cloakroom.

'It really is fantastic,' she enthused. 'Plasterwork

ceiling; lots of elegant gilt and glittering chandeliers.'

'In short, not exactly your average disco,' Chelsea teased.

Sandy grimaced. 'Trying to qualify as a doctor is one long hard slog without much time for discos or anything else. It doesn't help having most of the medical profession still firmly against women practitioners. They all seem to think you're going to rush off and get married the moment you're qualified—either that, or even worse, that you're using the training as a sort of husband-hunting ground.'

'Are you saying you don't want to get married?' Chelsea questioned lightly.

Sandy shook her head. 'Very much, and as you've probably guessed, to Tom, but that doesn't mean I wouldn't continue with my career. Have you known Slade long?' she asked, changing the subject.

Chelsea stiffened. 'No.' Had Tom told her about that scene with Slade? She discovered that she didn't want Sandy or anyone else thinking that she was simply another of Slade's women-friends.

'Oh, it's just that he was so worried about you when you were ill, insisting on looking after you himself, I thought . . .' She broke off and flushed.

'I think his concern sprang more from a desire to save Mrs Little any extra work than for me personally,' Chelsea replied evenly. 'Winter is a very busy time for a farmer's wife, isn't it?'

Sandy seemed to accept her explanation, but as they went to join the men Chelsea wondered if she had suspected that Slade had done it to protect her by, as he thought, keeping Chelsea away from Tom.

The ballroom was everything Sandy had claimed, and before too long they were the centre of a small group of people, most of whom seemed to know or have heard of Slade.

To her surprise he made a point of drawing her into his conversations, introducing her, and explaining what she was doing in the Borders. Everyone was very friendly, and Chelsea received several admiring requests to dance; the band stuck mainly to tried and traditional tunes, and although the evening was termed 'Young Farmers', there was a good spread of age groups. The only thing that spoiled her pleasure was the knowledge that she was far more sophisticatedly dressed than the other women, a fact which seemed to make her the cynosure of a good deal of male interest, which she found exceedingly uncomfortable.

A buffet supper had been set out in an adjoining room, but mouthwatering though it looked Chelsea found she seemed to have lost her appetite.

After everyone had eaten the mood of the evening seemed to change, set by the slower, more sensual numbers played by the band. Sandy looked frankly delighted when Tom bore her away to dance, and the dance floor filled up very quickly with couples obviously content to do little more than simply sway in one another's arms.

The coiled tension of her stomach muscles warned her of what to expect next, and it came as no surprise when Slade stood up and reached for her.

The evening was beginning to form a very

definite pattern, and Chelsea shivered as she considered its probable outcome. Without saying a word Slade was making it very plain that this time he was directing the course of events and that they would not be allowed to wander from the path he had chosen for them.

The main lights had been dimmed, and she trembled as Slade drew her into his arms, his embrace seemingly casual, but in reality tautly effective, making it impossible to break away from the close proximity of his body.

The pressure of his hand in the small of her back forced her body against him, each brush of thigh against thigh as they moved in time to the music sending shudders of awareness coursing through her. Her mouth felt dry and her heart as heavy as lead. There was no doubt in her mind now that Slade intended to reconstruct fully the events of the night they had met—nor of his intended finale. This time she could hardly flag down a passing taxi to take her home.

The music stopped. Slade's hands slid upwards to her shoulders, his mouth against her temple. It moved to her ear.

'The night we met,' he murmured softly, 'I looked at you and knew I had to make love to you, but you cheated on me, didn't you, Chelsea? You led me on with every enticing movement of your body, with every trick you've learned in the arms of who knows how many men.'

Her heart was thudding with painful intensity.

'Slade . . .' It hurt to say his name. Her throat was tight and aching with misery.

He lowered his head.

'You can't wait for us to be alone?' he murmured tauntingly. 'Is that it? That's what your body told me, the last time we danced like this.'

It was no use; she couldn't plead with him or make him understand. Her body sagged against him in defeat. Then the music stopped, and Sandy and Tom materialised at their side.

'Well, that's almost it,' Tom announced. 'Are you two ready to leave? It's a hard life for us farmers, we've got to be up before dawn—milking,' he added for Chelsea's benefit.

For one wild moment she was tempted to say that she had decided against returning to the Dower House and that she would stay at the hotel instead, but as though he read her mind, the hard tightening of Slade's fingers on her shoulder warned her that he was perfectly capable of announcing that he would stay with her. At least at the Dower House what happened between them would be mercifully cloaked in privacy. Suddenly she was too tired to fight him any longer; her bout of 'flu seemed to have depleted all her reserves of energy. Nothing she could say was going to convince him if his own contempt for her wasn't sufficient to overcome his need to restore his ego.

Telling herself that she despised him, Chelsea allowed him to guide her out to the Range Rover.

It was a crisp winter night. Just enough snow remained to lend a Christmas card prettiness to the hills, now laced with silver ice. A full moon shone from a breathtakingly clear sky. Chelsea couldn't remember when she had last seen the stars shine so brilliantly, and the air was cold enough to make her lungs ache when she breathed.

Once in the Range Rover Slade made no attempt to touch her. What had she expected? she wondered ironically; he probably knew as well as she did exactly the effect nervous apprehension was having on her nervous system; knew and enjoyed, she added bitterly. She was fast approaching the point where she was close to simply urging him appease his desire for retribution and then leave her alone.

The Dower House seemed to materialise all too quickly. While she was hesitating about prolonging the inevitable by inviting Tom and Sandy in for a cup of coffee, Slade calmly closed the Range Rover door, and turned her towards the house.

'Would you like a nightcap?' The smooth urbanity of the question jarred over her tensed nerves. She longed to scream at him to stop toying with her, but pride forced the bubble of hysteria down.

'No, thanks,' she replied as calmly as she could. 'I'm tired, I think I'll go straight to bed.'

She was just congratulating herself on having gained a temporary reprieve when he replied softly, 'What an excellent idea!' and before she could stop him he had bent to lift her in his arms. Just for a second his eyes were close enough for her to see the tiny golden flecks, molten tonight with what she thought must be anger, and then he was taking the stairs two at a time, and she knew with a sinking heart that tonight there was going to be no clamouring telephone; nothing in fact but the implacability she had read in his face as he bent towards her.

Inside his room he swung her to her feet and studied her for a moment before saying softly,

'Wise girl. I mean to have tonight what you so freely offered me once before, but on my terms, not yours, Chelsea, and they include complete abandonment of your body to me,' he told her huskily, 'not just the token emotion you assume for your other lovers, do you understand?'

How could she not do? She closed her eyes when she felt his fingers withdrawing the securing pins from her hair. It fell over her shoulders, cloaking them in a silky dark red swathe. Her dress followed the pins already scattered on the floor, her chin tilting defiantly as it fell to the floor with a soft whisper, exposing her body to what she had expected to be his cynically detached scrutiny. This wasn't desire, it was retribution, and yet the look in Slade's eyes as they roamed hotly over her body was one that turned her bones to liquid and sparked off a response deep inside her that she couldn't control.

'Chelsea!' Her name was muffled by the pressure of his mouth against her throat; the throbbing urgency of his thighs as he held her against him making a lie out of her mental assertion that he didn't desire her. He did, and with an intensity that evoked an answering response within her. She had told herself that his victory would be a hollow one, culminating in the unavoidable knowledge that before him there had been no other men. She had told herself that she knew him well enough to know that he would be mortified by his own lack of judgment, and that that would be her victory.

But she didn't know the man holding her with a hunger he wasn't trying to hide and that showed in the way his hands moulded her against him and his mouth savaged the soft skin of her throat, his heart thudding rapidly against her.

'Chelsea!' He said her name thickly, breathing unevenly, his skin flushed and damp. A great well of tenderness rose up inside her, as her arms reached up to draw him down against her breast, his smothered groan filling her with spiralling excitement as she reached down to smooth the dark hair.

'I want you!' He muttered it against the warm curve of her breasts, cupping them with his hands as his mouth lifted in urgent possession to her own.

Weakly Chelsea clung to him, sliding her hands inside his jacket, and then when she discovered that it wasn't enough, tugging impatiently at the tiny pearl buttons fastening his shirt. Slade seemed as eager as she was for her to touch his skin, his hands leaving her breasts to wrench open his shirt and discard it along with his jacket. As though they had hungered for the faintly abrasive touch of his hair-shadowed chest her nipples flowered instantly against him. Slade's response was to kiss her mouth deeply, and then she felt him lifting her and the depression of his bed beneath her.

'No . . .' He checked her faint movement to cling to him, looking down at her. 'The number of times I've imagined you like this, until I've thought I must be going out of my mind!'

His fingers sought and found the clip fastening her suspender belt. Her silky stockings were removed; Slade's lips lingered briefly on the soft, tender skin of her thighs, making her tremble slightly as he moved upwards, discarding the rest of his own clothes. His thighs with their dark covering of hair looked frighteningly powerful against the pale delicacy of her own. Fear and desire mingled in the pit of her stomach in an explosive mixture. She had expected Slade to take her with cold contempt, but instead he was lingering over each caress, arousing her as gently as though he knew that this was the first time she had experienced such intimacies. Her stomach muscles clenched protestingly as his mouth teased kisses over its tender swell. When he reached the barrier of her tiny briefs her husky 'No!' drew a surprised glance, but he made no comment, sliding his palms silkily up under her rib cage as he drew her down against him, his lips and tongue playing delicately with the aching burgeoning of her breasts until she writhed heatedly beneath him, her fingernails digging into the unyielding flesh of his back until he silenced her husky cries with the fierce pressure of his mouth.

When his hands returned to her briefs Chelsea had no thought of protesting. The lazy caress of his thumbs against her hips unleashed a frenzied need to arch her body against his and feel the heated urgency of its masculine thrust.

Beneath her palms his skin felt moist and hot, the muttered urgency of her name as it left his lips driving out any fear she might have felt as he slid between her thighs, lifting her up against him and burying his mouth in hers, inducing a hot velvet languor.

Dimly she was aware of some outside irritation,

and that Slade was aware of it too she could tell by
the sudden tensing of his body. Whatever it was
she didn't want it to intrude, and she wound her
arms round his neck, murmuring soft protests as
he released her mouth.

'History repeating itself with a vengeance,' he
muttered thickly, lifting his head. 'Someone's
knocking on the door, and by the sound of it
whoever it is doesn't intend to go quietly away.'

He slid off the bed, reaching for his trousers.
Chelsea sat up behind him, drawing her knees up
under her chin, shivering with reaction.

Slade turned suddenly to cup her chin, studying
her faintly bruised mouth and slumbrous expression.

'No need to look so disappointed,' he whispered.
'I'll be back, and the anticipation will only
heighten the pleasure.' He kissed her lightly but
with an assurance that told her he knew exactly
how much he had aroused her.

Pulling on a sweater, he fastened his trousers
and opened the door. Chelsea heard him going
downstairs and then the front door opening.
Straining her ears, she crept closer to the open door,
transfixed with shock when she heard Kirsty's
familiar voice saying enthusiastically, 'Slade, I
thought you were in New York! Is Chelsea here?'

Moving with a speed which was purely
instinctive, Chelsea gathered up her clothes and
fled to her own room. Kirsty! What on earth was
she doing here? Quickly finding her robe, she
pulled it on and belted it, as she hurried to the top
of the stairs, knowing that Slade was hardly likely
to tell Kirsty exactly what she had interrupted. At

the top of the stairs she stopped. Kirsty wasn't alone. There was a tall gangly fair-haired boy with her—

Kirsty glanced upwards and saw her standing at the head of the stairs, and a grin split her face.

'Chelsea! Were you asleep? Sorry to descend on you like this, but when I told Ma and Pa I was coming up here with Lance for a few days they said I had to come and see you.' She gave her aunt a mischievous grin, but before she could speak Slade was saying curtly,

'Look, it's nearly two in the morning. I suggest we all try and get some sleep for what's left of the night and then you can talk in the morning.'

Kirsty raised her eyebrows. 'Is he always as grumpy as this when he wakes up,' she questioned Chelsea, 'Or have we simply called at the wrong moment?'

'Kirsty!' Lance muttered warningly. 'Look, I'm sorry,' he apologised. 'We would have been here earlier, but my old banger broke down just outside Newcastle, and we had to get it fixed. I'm at university there and I told Kirsty we ought to stay there overnight and come on here tomorrow, but she wouldn't have it. Stubborn as a mule,' he added direfully, looking at her.

Kirsty laughed and put out her tongue. 'It runs in the family,' she said merrily, 'doesn't it, *Auntie*?'

Slade frowned. 'Chelsea is your aunt?'

'Yep, that's right,' Kirsty agreed cheerfully, 'Chelsea, you'll catch your death in that,' she commented practically. 'Why don't you tell us where we can sleep and we can talk in the morning?'

'You can have my bed,' Chelsea heard herself saying weakly as she avoided Slade's eyes. 'Er . . .'

'Lance can have the room next to mine,' Slade supplied. 'The bed's made up in there.'

'Come on,' Kirsty commanded, bounding up the stairs and grasping Chelsea's arm. 'I've got about a million messages to give you from Mum.' She bent her head and giggled as she looked down the flight of stairs at Slade. 'When Dad told her you were up here with Slade, she was like a mother hen whose chicken had wandered down a foxhole! You and I,' she told her aunt severely, 'have a lot to talk about.'

Once inside her room, Chelsea turned wearily to her niece. 'Kirsty, please,' she murmured, 'not tonight!'

Kirsty frowned and eyed her worriedly, 'Has Slade been giving you a bad time? Okay, okay, we'll talk about it in the morning,' she agreed when Chelsea's body sagged. 'But honestly, Chelsea—Mum I can understand, but I'd thought better of you. You must be losing your mind if you thought I'd ever be stupid enough to fall for Slade! He's way, way out of my league. I wasn't madly in love with him, stupid,' she said softly, 'I just wanted to try and persuade him to use his influence to make Mum and Dad see that just because acting didn't suit you it didn't mean that it wouldn't suit me. I got talking to him about it one day, and he was so nice and sympathetic I thought it wouldn't do any harm to try and work round to him dropping the odd hint to Dad about letting little birdies fly the nest, with him being Dad's boss and everything.'

'You weren't in love with him?'

Kirsty rolled her eyes and grinned. 'At my age? You must be joking! I'm not going to fall in love until I'm at least twenty-six. Oh, come on, Cee,' she protested, reverting to her childhood pet name for her aunt, 'you can't honestly believe I'm stupid enough to think a man of Slade's experience would be interested in a kid like me, nor inexperienced enough to run a mile if I thought he was?' she added wryly. 'He sees me as a kid, that's all. He's no Darren, you know,' she added gruffly. 'I thought you'd have been able to see that.'

Out of the mouths of babes, Chelsea thought wearily as she lay on the edge of sleep, Kirsty breathing evenly beside her. Of course he wasn't another Darren; and if she'd had the slightest scrap of sense she would have known it. She thought back, looking for indications of the same weakness in Slade which had marred Darren, but there had been none—quite the contrary. What she had done was to allow her prejudices and imagination into deceiving her that he was how she had wanted to see him and not how he was, even to the extent of leaping to the totally erroneous belief that Sandy was another of his 'victims'. In fact, if she was totally honest with herself Slade's only resemblance to Darren lay in her vulnerability to him, she admitted uncomfortably. The whole ridiculous charade at the party had been for nothing. She could have wept when she realised the truth. If it hadn't been for that she would never have come close enough to Slade to even think of falling in love with him; he would simply have been the owner of the Dower

House, and he would have seen her merely as a rather dull and boring woman who didn't attract him. How much heartache and pain she would have been saved if that had been the case! The heavy snowfalls had prevented her from finishing the tapestry as she had anticipated, but she estimated that by working non-stop she could finish inside a week. A week; it stretched interminably before her, a final obstacle to be overcome before she could make her exit from Slade's life—if possible without him discovering that she had been stupid enough to fall in love with him!

CHAPTER TEN

KIRSTY was still fast asleep when Chelsea woke up. Carefully avoiding waking the slumbering girl, she showered and dressed, telling herself that her anxiety to escape the bedroom without waking her had nothing to do with a cowardly desire to avoid any heart-to-heart with her niece.

She found Lance already in the kitchen filling the kettle. He gave Chelsea a tentative and slightly worried glance.

'I'm sorry we've burst in on you like this,' he apologised, 'but Kirsty's mum insisted that we came to see you when she knew we were going to be up in this direction.'

He went on to explain that one of his university friends was having a large twenty-first party in

Newcastle and that he and Kirsty were going to it.

Chelsea assured him that she was delighted to see them both. He was a very pleasant boy who seemed to have grown tremendously in the last year but who still possessed the gangly awkwardness of adolescence. Chelsea liked him and knew that Ann and Ralph did too. Without Ralph's sensible guiding hand she could quite see her sister encouraging Kirsty to settle down and marry her old playmate, but she reflected as she started to prepare breakfast, that Kirsty had her head screwed on far too firmly to get caught in the trap of a teenage marriage.

Kirsty and Slade arrived in the kitchen together just as she was cooking the bacon, and watching them together Chelsea wondered how she had ever been foolish enough to believe either of them to be romantically involved. Slade's manner towards her niece was that of an indulgent adult towards a boisterous, puppyish, much younger person. Kirsty was allowed to flirt with him, but only in such a manner that she knew exactly how far she was permitted to go and ventured no farther. The vast gulf that lay between his indulgence for Kirsty and his attitude towards her struck Chelsea immediately. Surely she wasn't jealous of her niece because Slade humoured and indulged her?

She busied herself with the breakfast, trying not to listen to the spontaneous bursts of laughter from the breakfast table; trying not to feel excluded from the charmed circle Slade seemed to have woven around the three of them.

Kirsty and Lance tucked appreciatively into the heaped plates she set before them.

'Mmm, lovely,' Kirsty sighed appreciatively. 'You're almost as good a cook as Mum. You'll never know what I had to go through to get her to agree to this weekend,' she added, assuming a hard-done-by air that brought a brief smile to Chelsea's lips. She knew how easily Kirsty could bend both her parents round her little finger. 'It was only when Dad came bursting in with the news that you were actually living in the same house as Slade that she suddenly had a change of heart. Poor Mum—she wasn't for telling me at first, but I soon wormed the whole thing out of her. It was absolutely hysterical really.' Kirsty's brown eyes laughed as she darted a mischievous look from Chelsea to Slade. 'Cee, I would have just loved to have been there when she coaxed you into that femme fatale act. I wondered what on earth you were playing at, wearing that fabulous dress and the new make-up.'

She wanted to vanish, Chelsea thought with mild hysteria; dissolve into thin air, disappear beneath the table, anything rather than face the look she knew must be in Slade's eyes.

Beneath the table Lance, more astute and observant than Kirsty, kicked her swiftly on the ankle. She paused, staring from her aunt's pale face to Slade's coolly unreadable one, her eyes widening in surprise.

'Oh, Cee,' she exclaimed apologetically, 'have I put my foot in it? Haven't you told him yet?' She turned impulsively to Slade, her hand on his arm as she smiled coaxingly up at him with a confidence Chelsea envied.

'Slade, don't be cross. Knowing my aunt she

must have hated pretending like that. You see, poor Mum thought that I was all poised for a heady affair with you. I soon put her right, of course. If only the silly thing had said something to me—but no. Off she goes worrying poor Cee and persuading her——'

'To make the heroic self-sacrifice of diverting my lustful intentions from you to herself,' Slade supplied dryly for her.

Completely unabashed, Kirsty grinned up at him, while Chelsea forced herself to drink her coffee as though nothing had happened, longing all the time to simply get up and run as far and as fast as she could away from Kirsty's humiliating disclosures.

'Look, Kirsty, I think it's time we made a move,' Lance murmured awkwardly,

'Any messages for Mum?' Kirsty asked Chelsea blithely, finishing her coffee. 'She told me to ask you when you were coming home.'

'Soon.' For the life of her Chelsea couldn't raise her head and look across the table. Tension coiled up inside her like a wire. If Slade had wanted retribution before what on earth must he think now that he had discovered that the whole thing had been nothing but a sham right from the start? How he must despise her! She reached for her coffee, but her hand shook so much she daren't lift the cup. Having witnessed at first hand his manner towards Kirsty, her own suppositions were both crude and shabby, and she couldn't understand how she had been stupid enough ever to believe them.

Right from the start she had recognised the fact

that Slade possessed a powerful attraction to her sex, but instead of drawing the sensible conclusion that that being the case he was hardly likely to interest himself in a seventeen-year-old girl she had bulldozed over all the warnings of common sense and convinced herself instead that he was another Darren, intent only on seeking childish adoration.

'Cee, are you all right?' She looked up from the table to find Kirsty watching her anxiously. 'You looked so pale. Are you okay?'

'She's still getting over a bad dose of 'flu,' Slade explained calmly before she could speak.

In the rush of goodbyes, there wasn't time for Chelsea to speak privately with her niece, but all the time she was conscious of Slade's intimidating presence and the knowledge that sooner or later she was going to have to face him.

She delayed the inevitable as long as she could, but eventually the small, dilapidated car of which Lance was so proud was disappearing down the road and the moment could be delayed no longer.

Quite what she expected Slade to say, she didn't know, but his speculative, 'So you're Kirsty's aunt?' and the look which accompanied it surprised her.

'Yes.' Her voice was betrayingly husky and uncertain as she turned away from him. They had been watching Kirsty and Lance leave from the study window, and now Chelsea was acutely conscious of Slade's presence behind her. Her legs seemed to have turned to jelly. She longed to turn round and face him, but somehow she just couldn't find the courage.

'The one who got involved with some married man?'

Her hand crept to her throat as though it could still the hectic pulse throbbing there, every vestige of colour leaving her face.

'Kirsty told you about that?' she asked incredulously.

'That and much, much more. You see, she was desperate to go to drama school and wanted me to intercede with her parents, but in fairness she wanted me to know the reasons they were against her going; that she was not merely the victim of parental arbitrariness—so she told me about you.'

It took less than a second for his words to sink in, and then bitterness welled up inside her, mixed with a pain and humiliation which made her long to escape.

Without looking at Slade she moved towards the door, but he barred it with his body.

'Chelsea!'

Shaking, she refused to obey the command implicit in his voice and look up at him. He knew everything; every tiny humiliating detail. She closed her eyes against the tears she knew were forming there. How could this have happened to her? She imagined Kirsty innocently confiding in him about her poor unfortunate aunt who had suffered an unfortunate romantic attachment in her teens, and because of it had remained a frigid virgin ever since. She could just imagine his reaction, his pitying amusement;

'Is it true?' he asked quietly.

His question seemed to shatter her bitterly fought for composure.

Tears flooded her eyes. 'Is what true?' she asked wildly. 'That I discovered the man I thought I loved didn't give a damn about me and only wanted me because he enjoyed sleeping with inexperienced virgins? That I allowed my sister to persuade me into behaving like a tramp to distract your attentions from Kirsty? That I escaped from my married lover's house with my virtue intact and my pride in tatters?'

'Damn you!' Slade swore unevenly, stunning her into silence. 'You know very well which . . .'

'They're all true,' she flung at him, 'even down to the fact which I'm sure Kirsty told you—that I'm still, after all these years, a virgin. Go on,' she told him, her voice high with defiance, 'laugh . . . I'm sure you're dying to!'

'Laugh?' He looked bitterly at her. 'I feel more like crying.'

Her breath seemed to leave her lungs on a painful gasp. She wanted to scream at him that she didn't want his pity, but she managed only to say fiercely, 'I don't want your tears!'

She tried to push past him, but he reached for her, grasping her upper arms and hauling her against him, the yellow specks in his eyes coagulating in a look that was fiercely molten.

'Who said they were for you? On the contrary I'd be crying for myself. The very first time I saw you I thought you were the sexiest thing I'd ever seen. I wanted to take you in my arms and never let you go. I couldn't believe my luck when you seemed to feel the same attraction, but I was speedily disillusioned. You certainly wanted me to think you wanted me, but there was no real desire there. I wanted to punish you, to hurt you, to make you respond to me, not whatever it was that had brought you to my side. I thought at the time it might have been greed, or even a purely feline desire to hang another scalp on your belt. You acted out your role perfectly, but no one can fake desire, and I knew you felt none for me; until we were in my apartment—it was like discovering a volcano under feet of ice, and then that damned phone rang and when I came back you were gone. No woman had ever done that to me before, and it infuriated me; all the more so because I knew you had responded to me. I asked Ralph about you, but he claimed he didn't know you. I tried to put you out of my mind, but you wouldn't leave. And then I came up here and discovered you in my own home, playing out what I thought was a falsely assumed role of demure innocence. I was right about the role-playing, but I'd got the roles the wrong way round, hadn't I?' he demanded grimly.

'I never thought I'd see you again,' Chelsea admitted defeatedly. 'I only went back with you to your flat because I was frightened that if I didn't you'd go back for Kirsty.'

'I ought to beat you for thinking that, although I suppose you thought you had just cause.' Slade pushed his hand tiredly through his hair. 'Now that I know the truth I can understand a hell of a lot better . . .'

'You mean you can see why I couldn't resist your lovemaking,' Chelsea said bitterly, 'now that you know I'm a frustrated, sex-starved spinster?'

He seemed to freeze, his eyes darkening, suddenly. 'Can't you?' he asked softly. His thumbs were stroking sensuously against her skin, and she shuddered with the pleasure his touch invoked. 'If that's true, I'm sorely tempted to carry you upstairs to my bed and keep you there until you've promised that you'll marry me. Sexual attraction might not be any substitute for love, but . . .'

Chelsea stared incredulously up at him. 'You'd marry me purely because you want me sexually?'

'I'd marry you because I simply can't envisage how I'm going to get through my life without you,' Slade corrected her savagely. 'From the moment you walked into my life it's been like that for me. When I came up here I told myself you were nothing but a little tramp; that I'd be wiser letting you have Tom if that was what you wanted. I tried to despise you because I knew no matter what you felt for Tom I could arouse you sexually. I told myself that if I possessed you I'd manage to exorcise you.'

'I thought you wanted to punish me, to teach me a lesson,' Chelsea half whispered. 'Over Christmas, when I came back from Darkwater and found that you were still here . . .'

'And promptly caused me some of the worst hours of my life,' Slade supplied. 'In more ways than one. First putting me through the torture of trying to find you in that damned blizzard. The only reason I didn't go to New York was because I was worried about you, all alone here, and what thanks do I get? First you run off and then you stretch my self-control to the ultimate limits, in a way I hope I never have to endure again,' he said huskily, shuddering as he drew her against him.

Vividly Chelsea remembered that evening and

the events which had followed.

'I wanted you so much,' she said painfully. 'But without love . . .'

'Sometimes one person's love is big enough for two,' Slade said softly.

She flushed then, thinking that all along he had known how she really felt about him; perhaps even before she had known herself.

'Slade . . .'

His finger touched her lips and she was surprised to feel how much it trembled.

'Don't say anything,' he urged her. 'I know you're sexually attracted to me, Chelsea, and from that I hope that a love will grow to match mine for you, but even if it doesn't I believe we have a chance together, a . . . What's the matter?' he demanded, as she suddenly stiffened and stared at him.

'You love me?'

He frowned. 'Oh, come on, Chelsea, no games, haven't I just spent the last fifteen minutes . . .' He broke off and stared at her. 'What the hell did you think I meant?'

'I thought you were talking about my love for you being enough for both of us,' she said softly. 'I thought you'd guessed . . . that you knew.'

'You love me?'

She could feel him tremble against her and felt a tiny surge of power.

'Very much,' she admitted simply. 'So much! Slade . . .'

She reached blindly for him, torn between laughter and tears when he took her mouth hungrily, possessing it with an urgency that sent her blood singing wildly through her veins.

'Thank goodness for Kirsty,' he said unevenly when he at last released her. 'If it hadn't been for her we could have gone on for ever, neither of us realising ... I nearly went mad that night you were lost in the snow,' he said abruptly. 'A saint couldn't have resisted,' he added huskily. 'I knew half of what you were doing was only induced by the brandy, and that's what stopped me in the end. I wanted you to love me, not just desire me, which infuriated me even further. Afterwards, I told myself that if I could turn the clock back to when we first met ... but even that didn't work, and excorcise you as I'd hoped. All it did was make me want you more than ever. Chelsea ...'

At the end of January Slade and Chelsea returned from their honeymoon in the Caribbean. Typically, Slade had been in no mind to wait once he knew she loved him. They had been married very quietly in Melchester, a mere ten days after Kirsty's visit. Ann had been at first embarrassed and then enchanted when she discovered who her new brother-in-law was to be.

Chelsea had stayed with her sister and Ralph until her marriage, at Slade's insistence. She had been a little chagrined and hurt, but on the first morning of their marriage, as they lay in bed together, Chelsea held possessively within Slade's arms as they listened to the sea pounding on the beach just outside the window of their villa, Slade had explained that he had deliberately kept some distance between them until they were married.

'Knowing it would be the first time for you, I

wanted to make it as perfect as possible,' he murmured against her throat, 'and if you'd continued to live at Darkwater, I couldn't have trusted myself to wait.'

There had been a lump in Chelsea's throat. He had made it perfect for her; by his patience and skill as much as the romantic surroundings he had chosen, tenderly fuelling her desire until the brief pain his possession brought was soon forgotten in the ecstasy that followed.

Now they were back at Darkwater and the old house was almost ready for opening to the public. Mrs Rudge had been dismissed and a girl from the village came in to help with the housework. Chelsea preferred it that way because it meant that they could spend their evenings completely alone.

'Looks good, doesn't it?' Slade commented, as they both studied the tapestry, which was now mounted under glass in the long gallery.

'Fantastic,' Chelsea agreed, her eyes drawn to the golden-haired girl she had so carefully worked on, a small smile tugging at the corners of her mouth.

'All right,' Slade grinned, reading her mind, 'so I was wrong about her.'

'I knew all along that she really loved him,' Chelsea said smugly. 'Feminine intuition!'

She had been thrilled and delighted the day Slade came home to tell her that from some documents the Trust had discovered in the house it was apparent Damask had loved her Crusader and that apparently he had been deceived by his brother, just as Chelsea had imagined, that same

brother confessing his crime to his priest on his
deathbed.

With Slade's arm around her waist, Chelsea
leaned blissfully against him. She could still hardly
believe that they were married, that he loved her;
although . . . Another smile tugged at her lips and
Slade smiled down at her,

'How's your intuition working now, Mrs
Ashford?' he murmured softly. 'If it doesn't tell
you that your husband is extremely anxious to
make love to you then it's badly at fault.'

Her laughter was silenced beneath his mouth.
Her arms crept up round his, her fingers
tightening in his hair as the pressure of his mouth
deepened. Momentarily she felt a haunting
sadness for Damask, but then Slade claimed all
her attention, and she responded eagerly to the
slow seduction of his kiss and the pleasure she
knew would follow.

Harlequin® Plus

HOW BOXING DAY GOT ITS NAME

December 26, the day after Christmas, is called Boxing Day. To many people, it's a welcome rest after all the weeks of Christmas preparation and sometimes hectic celebrations. For hundreds of years gifts were conferred on Boxing Day, but the occasion has had slightly different meanings for people in different centuries.

In medieval times, the day after Christmas was known as St. Stephen's Day. Marked by feasting and acts of charity, this day was used by lords and ladies of the great manor houses to give their farmer tenants coal and provisions. During the weeks just before Christmas, little clay boxes with slots for coins were placed in churches to collect donations for the poor. Because these boxes were broken open and the contents distributed on St. Stephen's, the day came to be called Boxing Day.

In Victorian England, Boxing Day celebrations took on a slightly different form—although the charitable intent was the same. Members of the upper classes put food and drink into boxes for the poor of their parishes, visiting workhouses and hostels to distribute these gifts. By 1871, Boxing Day celebrations had become so popular that the day was made a holiday by an act of Parliament.

And now, with department stores holding after-Christmas clearance sales, Boxing Day may take on yet another connotation—all those armloads of boxes and parcels we carry home from the department stores after reaping the bargains!